★

In the middle of act 2, scene 4, Orsino had just asked Cesario, "And what's her history?"

Sally Luther replied, "A blank, my lord: she's never told her love, but let concealment i' th' bud feed on her."

Suddenly she clutched at her throat and started gagging. She fell down onto the wet stage.

After what seemed an age, an ambulance made it across the muddy grounds of Chailey Ferrars to pick up the invalid and take her to the local hospital.

And on the next morning's radio and television news bulletins it was announced that Sally Luther was dead.

★

"This is a fine, funny British mystery with a likable protagonist."

—*West County Times, CA*

SIMON BRETT

Sicken and So Die

WORLDWIDE®

TORONTO • NEW YORK • LONDON
AMSTERDAM • PARIS • SYDNEY • HAMBURG
STOCKHOLM • ATHENS • TOKYO • MILAN
MADRID • WARSAW • BUDAPEST • AUCKLAND

SICKEN AND SO DIE

A Worldwide Mystery/January 1998

This edition is reprinted by arrangement
with Scribner, an imprint of Simon & Schuster, Inc.

ISBN 0-373-26262-0

To Michael

ONE

THINGS WERE ACTUALLY going rather well for Charles Paris. Basically, it was a matter of work. He had work, he was in work, he was working. For an actor, a job is the switch that turns the personality on to full power. Without it Charles Paris existed. He had all the components of himself—his cynicism, his gloom, his apologetic lusts, his drinking, his deflated air of defeat. But with a job all those elements fused and he was energized, sustained by a galvanic charge that even incorporated optimism.

What was more, he was doing good work. He was playing a good part in what promised to be a good production of a good play. *Twelfth Night* by William Shakespeare—plays don't come a lot better than that. Nor, for a slightly frayed, unraveling actor in his late fifties, do parts come a lot better than Sir Toby Belch.

Playing a major Shakespearean role made Charles feel that perhaps his career had come back on course—or perhaps finally come on course. The theatre offers no obvious career structure—indeed its ups and downs make investing in the National Lottery look a secure bet—but there are certain milestones to which all actors aspire. To play Sir Toby Belch in one's late fifties is a necessary notch carved on the bedpost of a career, a qualification that opens up the possibility of a Henry IV, a Prospero, or even the ultimate prize of a Lear, in one's sixties.

Charles had played big parts in Shakespeare before, but the time or the production had never been right. He had been too young when cast as Macbeth, badly directed as Henry V, and as for his leading role in *Julius Caesar*...well, even Charles himself agreed with the estimation of the *Lancashire Evening Post* that "here was a Mark Antony to whom even Vincent van Gogh wouldn't have lent an ear."

But this *Twelfth Night* felt right. Only a week into a four-week rehearsal period, but the whole production had a glow of confidence about it, a growing conviction among the company that they were involved in a show that was going to be successful.

This was something of a surprise because the director was not the most dynamic in the history of the theatre. In fact, Charles Paris had always considered Gavin Scholes rather ineffectual. They'd worked together a good few times, most recently on *Macbeth* at the Pinero Theatre, Warminster, where Gavin had been artistic director.

Charles had assumed that, at the end of his contract there, Gavin would have retired to nurse his hypochondria and irritable bowel syndrome; but the director had confounded expectations by developing a very successful subsequent career as a freelance. This was proof once again that charisma and innovation in the world of theatre count for less than good old-fashioned competence. Gavin Scholes's productions might not set the world on fire, but they told their stories clearly, came in on time, and stayed within their budgets. These were virtues that appealed to production companies.

The current *Twelfth Night* was being mounted by Asphodel Productions, a touring management who had risen to prominence during the previous five years. Their recipe of simply narrated classics—frequently Shakespeare and almost always A-level set texts—had proved extremely successful. Clever, uncluttered set design had made their productions mobile and suitable for all kinds of different performance spaces. One week they'd appear in a conventional theatre, the next a school gymnasium, then a library, a leisure center, a church hall, or a warehouse. As the company's fame spread, so did the range of their touring venues, which now included foreign destinations.

They were poised for greater recognition. They needed one breakthrough production to capture the attention of the national press, and Asphodel's name would be firmly fixed on the British cultural map.

The designated tour for *Twelfth Night* was characteristic of the company's current outreach. It began early August. The first six performances would be open air, in the gardens of Chailey Ferrars, an Elizabethan mansion in Hertfordshire; they would be presented as part of the ten-day Great Wensham Festival.

Thereafter the show would move on to a studio theatre in Norwich for two weeks. Seven performances in a Billericay leisure center would be followed by three in a public school's own theatre near Crawley and three on the boarded-over swimming pool of a

Reading comprehensive. After a week in a converted Methodist chapel near Cheltenham, the company had a few days' break before the highspot of the tour—three performances at the University of Olomouc in the Czech Republic. Back in England, weeks in a former corn exchange in Warwick, a temperance hall in Swindon, and a prefabricated sports dome in Aldershot would then climax in the relatively sedate booking of three weeks back at Gavin Scholes's former base, the Pinero Theatre in Warminster.

For Charles Paris all of this represented, with rehearsals, the rare phenomenon of more than four months of guaranteed work. It also offered the prospect of recapturing the excitement of constant change, which had largely vanished from the theatre since the demise of weekly rep.

As well as being cautious in his interpretation of plays, Gavin Scholes was also conservative in his casting. He liked working with people he knew, their familiarity cushioning him against the potential "difficulty" of actors he didn't know. When he had to introduce new members into this charmed circle, he favored performers suggested by actors he did know. He particularly liked to use recommended young actors at the beginning of their careers; they were eager and biddable, and unlikely to question the authority of their director.

Charles Paris recognized that this approach was uninventive and prevented Gavin's productions from reaching the creative heights, but the system was not one he was going to complain about, since he was one of its beneficiaries. However suitable Charles Paris might be for Sir Toby Belch, he couldn't see the National or the RSC suddenly going out on a limb and casting him in the role. They'd go for someone much more starry and voguish. Come to that, Charles couldn't see himself getting the part in any lesser company where an old pals' act was not in operation.

So he was all in favor of Gavin Scholes's "safety first" casting policy. It brought another benefit too; there were other members of the *Twelfth Night* company with whom Charles had worked before, which is always—or, depending on the individuals involved, perhaps *usually* would be a better adverb—a comfort to any actor. Two of the cast of Gavin's *Macbeth* were also in the new production.

Russ Lavery had come a long way since playing Fleance and Young Siward in Warminster. That had been his first job in the theatre, and his undoubted talent had been obscured then by a callow, puppyish approach to "the business." But four or five years of solid stage and small television parts had preceded the breakthrough when he'd been cast as Dr. Mick Hobson in ITV's *Air-Sea Rescue.*

The show, now into its third series and showing no sign of flagging in the ratings, had turned a young actor of identical talent to at least a hundred of his contemporaries into a household name and a household face. *Air-Sea Rescue* had brought Russ Lavery all of the bonuses of money from escalating fees and foreign repeats, fan mail from half the nation's teenage girls, lucrative offers for personal appearances and voice-overs, and the possibility of saying in interviews that "I get sent lots of scripts, but I don't like to commit myself to a project unless I feel it is a really exceptional piece of work."

It also enabled him to say in interviews that "I really feel the need to get back to my theatrical roots," which explained his appearance in Gavin Scholes's *Twelfth Night*. The fact that he was playing the relatively small and ungrateful part of Sebastian did his image no harm at all. Rather, it demonstrated what an unstarry star Russ Lavery was, and how serious was his dedication to his art. The presence of a well-known television name in the cast of *Twelfth Night* wouldn't do any harm at the box office, either.

The other familiar face in the company provided Charles Paris with even greater cause for celebration. John B. Murgatroyd was an actor against whom Charles had frequently bumped in his theatrical career, and the experience had always been a delightful one. John B. was a clown, a great giggler, in whose company Charles had frequently been reduced to incapable hysterics and behavior that would be judged immature in a primary school. John B. was a great person to have around any production.

In the Warminster *Macbeth* he had given his distinctive and stunningly versatile interpretations of both Lennox and the First Murderer. In *Twelfth Night* he was playing Sir Andrew Aguecheek. Since most of Sir Toby Belch's scenes included the wan and winsome knight, Charles was relishing the prospect of building up his double act with John B. onstage as well as off.

AND IT WASN'T JUST the work that was going well. For once, Charles Paris's emotional life was also looking promising. He wasn't experiencing the tense, manic uncertainty of a new love affair, but the solid comfort of an old one.

Charles had been married to Frances for twelve years before he finally walked out. He had used all kinds of justifications, about the incompatibility of an actor's lifestyle with the institution of marriage, about the need for them both to develop outside the claustrophobia of cohabitation, but the real motive for his departure had been self-punishment. He'd been having affairs away from home, and he felt guilty about them. Walking out on Frances—and their daughter, Juliet—had been a kind of public penance for his misdemeanors.

It had also, he'd hoped at the time, been a bid for freedom. On his own, he would be able to follow up on the emotional hints and half-chances that other women offered. What he'd done was hurtful, but necessary to his fulfilling the imperatives of his personality. Marriage had been part of his growth, but a part that he had outgrown.

Of course, it hadn't worked out like that. The freedom for which he had given up Frances proved illusory. Yes, he followed up on the other women. He had some good sex and some bad sex, he made some good friends, he even at times imagined himself in love, but all the relationships left him ultimately empty. There was still a void in his life that only Frances could fill.

He'd worried the situation through in his head more

times than he cared to count and almost always came back to the same basic problem. He liked Frances.

That was aside from loving her, which he sometimes did, or from time to time feeling toward her an infuriation that qualified as hatred. But the liking remained constant; that was the invisible chain that held him to her.

For a total split from a lover, there needs to be a two-way pressure. Not just the overwhelming attraction for the new love object, but also a distaste for the old. Constant comparisons then become inevitable. The new love is not only wonderful, she is also so much more wonderful than the one I am leaving. In fact, when I catalog the faults, deficiencies, and inadequacies of the old love, the only point remarkable is that I stayed with her so long. Why did I put up with someone so unsuitable for all that time?

But such a natural process of fission is rendered inoperable when you still *like* the old love, when you worry about her, think about her, want to discuss things with her. The loving and the hating are relatively easy to cope with; it's the liking that makes the whole thing impossible.

And that, Charles had come to realize ruefully, was the state of play in his relationship with his wife. Whatever else there might be happening in his sex life—and at times there had been quite a bit—he still felt linked to Frances.

Whether she felt the same obligation, he was never quite sure. And even in those moments when he did feel quite sure, he was also aware of how much she resented the encumbrance. At times she seemed very distant from him. At times he knew for certain that she had had other men. But did the fact that none of those had gone the distance mean that Frances's relationships were hobbled by the same restrictions that cramped his own?

Charles Paris knew that he wanted a closer intimacy with his wife, but he could never be certain how much she shared that ambition.

The circumspection of her attitude was not without justification. Charles could not claim to be the most assiduous of men in the protocol of marriage. Even if one were to put on one side the fact of his having walked out on his wife—and he could recognize that that was a significant blot on the marital copybook—his behavior since that time would not always have inspired confidence in a potential partner.

He did have a tendency to get distracted. The intention to ring Frances, make contact, fix to meet up, was always there, but when he got involved in a production, when he was away for a while, it was remarkable how the weeks—and even the months—could slip past without his acting on that intention.

There had also been one or two regrettable incidents when he had fixed a rendezvous and been prevented by circumstance, or occasionally drink, from fulfilling his part of the arrangement—the small matter of turning up at the agreed place at the agreed time.

Charles could fully sympathize with Frances's skepticism when he spoke of a closer future between them.

And it wasn't as if she didn't have a full life. Now

independent with her own flat in Highgate, she had risen through the educational system to be headmistress of a girls school. She was a caring mother and a solicitous grandmother. What possible incentive could she have to make room in her well-ordered life for a man whose moody personality took over any environment like a wet Labrador?

And yet at the moment she was making room in her life for Charles, and at the moment the experiment seemed to be working.

It was all down to the builders, really. When he'd left Frances, Charles had moved into a dingy and soulless bed-sitter in Hereford Road, "just in the short term, you know, till I find somewhere more suitable," and he was still there. Or at least he would still have been there had not the new landlord of the house embarked on the long-overdue transformation of the bed-sitters into "studio flats."

Once the work was completed, the existing tenants would be given first refusal to continue residency at increased rents, but obviously all had to move out while the builders gutted the property. Charles, remarkably, had moved in with Frances.

It was convenient—particularly since the *Twelfth Night* rehearsals were taking place in a church hall in Willesden. It was also logical—or it would have been for a couple whose marital history was less checkered.

But the most astonishing thing about the arrangement was that it seemed to be working. They were actually getting on rather well.

Maybe it was age. Maybe they had both matured

and could be more tolerant of each other. Maybe both had learned from and been enriched by the traumas of their long separation.

The best part for Charles was that Frances had let him back into her bed. The ease and familiarity of their lovemaking glowed in him through the days like a personal heart-warmer. He didn't feel lonely. It was a long time since he hadn't felt lonely. A long time since he had had someone to go home to at the end of the day.

One unexpected side effect of this domesticity was that Charles was drinking less. The automatic loose-end recourse to the pub at the end of rehearsals seemed less imperative, and the too many nightcaps of Bell's to deaden the end of the day were no longer necessary. He and Frances would share a bottle of wine over dinner, but often that was the sum total of his day's intake. For Charles Paris, that made quite a change.

His new circumstances generally made quite a change.

It was early days, mind. Less than two weeks they'd been cohabiting, and neither of them wanted to threaten the fragility of what was happening by talking about it.

Promising, though. Somehow, Charles felt confident the thoughts going through Frances's mind matched his own. It wasn't too late for them still to make something of their lives together.

Yes, Charles Paris reflected, as the train sped toward Great Wensham and the *Twelfth Night* photo call, things are actually going rather well.

TWO

THE FORMAL Elizabethan gardens of Chailey Ferrars could have been designed as a setting for *Twelfth Night*. Their geometric patterns offered a choice of avenues down which Malvolio could walk. Their statuary, low walls, and neatly clipped box trees offered manifold hiding places from which Sir Toby Belch, Sir Andrew Aguecheek, and Fabian could observe the steward picking up the letter from "The Fortunate-Unhappy" and falling for Maria's trick to make him believe his mistress Olivia loved him.

The Asphodel production of the play was not to be performed in the formal gardens, however. They were far too precious, far too carefully maintained, to be overrun by actors and picnic-toting members of the public. The acting area for *Twelfth Night* was farther away from the house, in a walled field at one end of which a natural amphitheatrical shape had been enhanced by the construction of a grass-covered mound and the planting of a semicircle of trees around it. For performances a wooden stage was erected on the mound and the backstage area cordoned off with hessian screens.

It was the Chailey Ferrars trustees who imposed conditions on which parts of the estate could be used. They were a body of men and women of prelapsarian conservatism, who saw it as their God-given mission to resist every proposed change to the house or gardens. They would really have liked the public excluded totally from the premises, but had grudgingly been forced to accept the financial necessity of paying visitors.

At first the trustees had resisted the overtures of the Great Wensham Festival Society to stage plays at Chailey Ferrars. But the third year, having seen how much other businesses had benefited from the new custom attracted by the Festival, they had agreed to very limited access to the grounds for two public performances of *Much Ado About Nothing*. Again grudgingly, they had to concede that the experiment had not led to wholesale vandalism of their precious property, and that it had indeed proved rather profitable to the Trust, as well as being an artistic success.

From then on the Chailey Ferrars Shakespeare had become a regular feature—indeed the main focus—of the Great Wensham Festival, though the trustees never allowed its continuance to be taken for granted. Each year the Festival director, Julian Roxborough-Smith—or in the event his administrator, Moira Handley—had to go through an elaborate square dance of application and supplication until the trustees—with an ever-increasing number of cautions and provisos—agreed to let the Chailey Ferrars grounds be used for yet another Shakespearean production.

It was a measure of Moira Handley's skillful management of the trustees that, though there would never be any possibility of the play's being staged in the

formal gardens, she had elicited permission for the
Twelfth Night photo call to be held there.

As an even greater concession, the trustees had allowed the accompanying press conference to be con-
ducted in the Chailey Ferrars dining room. The mag-
nitude of this honor was continuously emphasized,
though, since Asphodel was being forced to pay well
over the odds for the Chailey Ferrars in-house catering
services, the trustees' attitude did seem a little hypo-
critical.

Still, Charles Paris wasn't that worried. A photo call
and a press conference had to mean a few free drinks.

HE HAD BEEN unperturbed by the prospect of a visit
to Great Wensham, though many of the other company
members had made a big fuss about it. Gavin Scholes
objected to losing a day's rehearsal, even though his
presence at the press conference was written into the
contract between Asphodel and the Great Wensham
Festival. His wardrobe mistress resented the demand
for costumes to be worn at the photo call; she grumbled that it was only local press, anyway, surely they
could be fobbed off with rehearsal stills. But again a
fully dressed on-site photo call was written into the
contract.

These complaints, however, were as nothing to
those raised by the cast. Few of the principals wanted
to drag out to Great Wensham for some bloody photo
call; they regarded a day without rehearsals as a day
off, and at the beginning of four months' intensive
work they weren't going to miss out on that.

Russ Lavery was particularly vehement in his refusal when Gavin Scholes tried to cajole him into being part of the outing. Up until that point, he had been very meek and unstarry at rehearsal—except for one violent blowup with the wardrobe mistress, who'd wanted to give Viola's and Sebastian's costumes shorter sleeves than Russ Lavery thought appropriate. Needless to say, the star had won; the sleeves were lengthened.

But the press conference prompted another tantrum. Russ's agent, the actor explained, had set up a meeting for that day with a Hollywood director who'd got a project Russ might be interested in. When Gavin rather tentatively pointed out that "availability for promotion of the production" was written into Russ's contract, Gavin was nearly blown out of the water.

"I don't have to make myself available for bloody local hacks!" the star of *Air-Sea Rescue* stormed. "My publicist and I spend most of our time *avoiding* publicity, not courting it."

"It's not going to be just local coverage," Gavin asserted. "The Festival press officer I spoke to said they've invited all the nationals as well."

"I don't care if they've invited the pope, Barbra Streisand, and Nelson Mandela," said Russ Lavery. "*I* won't be there."

So the party who actually did attend the photo call and press conference were the amenable ones who tended not to make a fuss, such as Charles Paris and Tottie Roundwood, the actress who was playing Maria; and those who were desperate for publicity in whatever form it came—Vasile Bogdan, who played Fabian, Sally Luther, the production's Viola, and Talya Northcott, for whom *Twelfth Night* was her first professional job.

Talya had been cast in the nonspeaking role of Olivia's Handmaiden, with the additional responsibility of understudying all three female parts. For someone so new to the profession, just working in the theatre was profoundly exciting. And any newspaper picture of her in costume would be religiously snipped out and scrapbooked by the worshiping "Mummy" to whom her conversation frequently reverted.

Vasile Bogdan, a gloweringly handsome, dark-haired actor in his twenties, may have had an obscure European name, but he spoke without any trace of an accent. He was fiercely ambitious, and his opinion of his talents manifested itself in a slight contempt for the rest of the company. His *Twelfth Night* casting in the ungrateful role of Fabian was a stage through which he considered himself only to be passing briefly on his way to greater things. An opportunity to get his photograph in a newspaper—any newspaper—was not one that at this stage of his career he would ever pass up.

Sally Luther's relationship with the publicity machine was more complex. In her early twenties she had been the tabloids' darling. A pretty blond ingenue, she had been effortlessly cast straight out of drama school as one of the leads in the ITV sitcom *Up To No Good*. In that show she had charmed the nation through four series and become a familiar presence failing to answer the questions on showbiz quizzes, guesting daffily on game shows, and manning phone lines on charity telethons. She described the interior of her flat to color supplements, her kind of day to the *Radio Times,* and her first kiss to teenage magazines. She had all the trappings of stardom—a fan club, a rose named after her, and even the unwanted attentions of obsessive fan letters and a mysterious stalker. The public loved her, she could do no wrong, and she made a very good living.

Sally Luther's fall from this state of grace was not dramatic. No messy breakups from famous boyfriends, no arrests for drunken driving, no allegations of drug abuse. She just slowly dropped out of the public consciousness. *Up To No Good* was not recommissioned for a fifth series. The pilot for a new Sally Luther sitcom was rejected. Guest appearances in other sitcoms became more spaced out and finally dried up.

The public did not fall out of love with Sally Luther; they simply forgot about her. Without a weekly reminder of her face on their television screens, she slipped imperceptibly out of the collective memory.

She wasn't out of work. She wasn't broke. She didn't crack up. She was just brought up hard against the fact that she'd had a lucky start, and if she was going to continue in the business, then she'd have to rebuild her career from scratch.

And she'd have to rebuild it from different elements. The baby face that had floated her through her early twenties had grown harder and more lined. The natural blond of her hair had darkened to a light brown. She could of course have kept the color artificially, but decided not to. The new Sally Luther was not going to be a clone of the old.

She had never been as stupid as she appeared on the screen. She applied her considerable intelligence and pragmatism to starting again.

Charles Paris admired the determination with which Sally Luther had hit the comeback trail. She had immersed herself in stage work, learning the basics of a trade that her television success had bypassed. She had taken small parts in out-of-the-way theatres, slowly building competence and experience. She had worked her way up from being a pretty face to a respectable actress, and the Asphodel Productions' Viola was the highest point yet of her reconstituted career.

It was Charles's secret opinion that Sally Luther, even with all her grafting away, was not really a good enough actress to play Viola. But he respected her professionalism and enjoyed working with her.

THE TRUSTEES of Chailey Ferrars grudgingly—it was the adverb with which they performed their every action—allowed the *Twelfth Night* cast a small room off the ground-floor administrative office in which to change. So, amidst coffee and photocopying machines, and in cramped proximity to Vasile Bogdan and the three—mercifully small—actresses, Charles Paris donned his Sir Toby Belch costume.

He was pleased that Gavin Scholes was doing the play in what he, Charles, thought of as the ''right'' period—in other words, contemporary with when it had been written. Charles Paris had had enough of gimmicky productions of Shakespeare. He'd been in a 1920s flapper-style *Love's Labour's Lost;* he'd worn cutoff jeans as Bardolph in *Henry V,* a pin-striped suit as one of the Tribunes in *Coriolanus,* a hippie caftan as Lancelot Gobbo, and even a tutu in a hopelessly misconceived cross-dressing *All's Well....* ("All's Well That Ends Well, but here was a production which neither started nor ended well. In fact, so far as this critic's concerned, it would have ended much better three hours before it actually did."—*Financial Times*)

What a relief, after all that, to be playing Shakespeare in appropriate dress. Gavin Scholes's lack of imagination did have its advantages.

ALSO, FOR ONCE, Charles actually had a new costume. For most period productions of his career he'd been dressed in something hired from a theatrical costumier or tatted together from whatever could be found in wardrobe. He'd become accustomed to other men's clothes, to walking around in the aura—or, in certain regrettable instances, the smell—of another actor.

But Asphodel employed a pukka costume designer for all their shows. This was partly so that the costumes could reflect a production design concept, but there were practical reasons too. A four-month engagement justified the expense of specially made costumes, and the company was also shrewdly building up its own wardrobe stock, which was increasingly hired out to other managements. There were astute business brains behind Asphodel Productions.

Charles Paris liked his Sir Toby Belch costume. The designer's overall theme was muted grays and silver, which reflected *Twelfth Night*'s underlying melancholy—and also pointed up even more the virulent shock of Malvolio's yellow cross-gartering.

And the designer had not succumbed to the common error of making Sir Toby scruffy. The man was a gentleman of the court, after all, so Charles Paris was dressed in charcoal velvet doublet and hose, piped with silver and slashed with oyster-colored silk. He had a silver-frosted ruff and a small charcoal hat with a fluffy, pale gray feather. As Charles donned the costume in the Chailey Ferrars office, he did feel rather pleased with himself.

He felt particularly pleased that the costume's generous cut rendered his own paunch inadequate and forced him actually to pad for the role. This gave Charles a spurious sense of righteousness, as did the fact that he also had to redden his face with makeup. The Bell's whiskey may have taken its toll, but it had not yet sufficiently ravaged his complexion for him to play Sir Toby without cosmetic help. All encouraging stuff.

As well as a specially made costume, Charles had had a customized beard constructed by Wig Creations, and this too gave him a sense of being pampered. As he peered into the tiny mirror, the familiar alcohol smell of spirit gum in his nostrils, and pressed Sir Toby's luxuriant mustache onto his upper lip, Charles Paris felt good.

His self-satisfaction must have expressed itself in

his body language because Tottie Roundwood, reaching round to pull up the zip of her jet-black Maria costume, grinned and said, "Yes, very handsome indeed."

Charles grinned back. "Let me." He reached across to help her with the zip.

Tottie Roundwood was probably round the fifty mark, short, plumpish, dark hair beginning to be streaked with gray. She was one of those actresses capable of enormous fireworks onstage, but quiet and reserved the rest of the time. Charles liked her, though he knew little about her, except that she was interested in some system of alternative medicine. Reflexology? Healing? Homeopathy? One of those, anyway, he couldn't remember.

He patted her shoulder to indicate that the dress was secure and reflected on the total lack of sexual charge the contact gave him. Actors are so used to sharing dressing rooms with actresses that, in that context, both almost lose all sexual identity. Charles couldn't help observing that Sally Luther still had a pretty good body, though.

To his surprise, this little glancing thought made him feel guilty. There was a tiny pang of disloyalty to Frances, with whom he'd made tender and extended love the night before. Obviously his wife's body had to give Sally Luther's twenty years, but it was still looking pretty terrific. And, he concluded virtuously after a covert look at Talya Northcott slipping into her costume, I don't fancy that really young one at all.

Neat little figure, nice blond hair maybe, but it doesn't do a thing for me.

Goodness, thought Charles Paris, I am changing. If this goes on, I'll soon be positively uxorious.

Gavin Scholes came bustling into the office. "Okay, are you set? The press—such as they are—are all here, and we're ready to go."

THREE

"...BUT PERHAPS the Shakespeare is the jewel in our crown—though of course the Great Wensham Festival is a crown of many jewels—as you will be able to see from the press releases that are on the table over there. Anyway, we of the Festival Society are absolutely delighted to welcome, for the third year running, Asphodel Productions. I'm sure you all enjoyed their *Midsummer Night's Dream* and *As You Like It,* and I am confident that we can look forward to the same qualities of robust storytelling in this year's *Twelfth Night*—whose performance, incidentally, is made possible by the generous sponsorship of Mutual Rel—"

At a warning cough from a dark-haired woman beside him, the Festival director, Julian Roxborough-Smith, hastily corrected himself.

"—of a variety of national and local businesses, which you will find listed in the press release. I would also like to acknowledge at this point the invaluable contribution made by Hertfordshire Arts Network, without which the scope of the Great Wensham Festival would be considerably less broad.

"As you see, some members of the *Twelfth Night* cast have been good enough to join us today. Yes, they are in costume—those aren't their normal street clothes." A little pause for the even littler joke. No reaction. "But before we become more informal and you get a chance to chat to them, I'm going to call on *Twelfth Night*'s director to say a few words about the production. Ladies and gentlemen of the press, will you please welcome—Mr. Gavin Scholes."

"Lady and gentleman of the press" might have been more accurate, Charles reflected. Though there were lavish amounts of sandwiches and other snacks—and a gratifying number of wine bottles—laid out in the dining room of Chailey Ferrars for the press conference, there did seem to be a marked lack of press.

A bored-looking man in his fifties held a notebook and pencil, but had not yet heard anything he deemed worthy of recording; and an earnest-looking girl, barely out of her teens, pointed a cassette player with great concentration at whoever happened to be speaking. Otherwise, a single photographer, burdened down by a shoulder bag of camera impedimenta, shifted from one foot to the other at the back of the hall, with the expression of someone who should already have moved on to cover the local primary school's Wildfowl Week.

Julian Roxborough-Smith's address had not been likely to stir much excitement among the press, even if more of them had been present. It was not what he said that was uncharismatic; it was the manner of his saying it. The Festival director had one of those languid, slightly theatrical voices that suggests he is doing everyone a favor by speaking at all and imparts an unintentional tinge of contempt to everything. He was a tall man pushing sixty and turning to fat. His sandy hair was thinning. He wore a suit in broad pinstripe. The thick-framed glasses and spotted bow tie seemed to accentuate rather than obscure the nondescript nature of his face.

"Twelfth Night," Gavin Scholes began, "is one of the most charming of Shakespeare's comedies, and yet at the same time it is one of the darkest. The treatment meted out to Malvolio alone prevents the play from being the jolly romp which it is sometimes portrayed...as," he added uneasily, having got a little lost in his syntax. "And in my production I have deliberately emphasized the—"

"Look, if you want to have any photographs, we're going to have to do them now," a harsh voice interrupted from the back of the dining hall. "I'm already running late."

Since with no visual record the press conference would be even more of a nonevent than it was already, the photographer's bad manners won the day, and the five costumed cast members were trooped out to the formal gardens to strike Elizabethan poses against the statuary.

They were shepherded by a small, anxious woman who had identified herself earlier as Pauline Monkton, press officer for the Great Wensham Festival. She kept apologizing for the lack of press at the conference, and while apologies were certainly in order, the way she went on about it quickly became wearing.

"I mean, I don't know what you can *do*," she said plaintively. "They all got invited—the nationals and everything. They had their invitations *weeks* ago. And they did *say* RSVP, but do you know, hardly any of them have even *bothered* to reply. I mean, once you've invited them and given them all the information, well, what else can you *do?*''

Hire a professional publicist or public relations company, would have been Charles's answer. He had encountered the fatal touch of the amateur at other arts festivals, and he knew it almost never worked. Publicity is a hard-nosed, cutthroat business; any number of highly sophisticated organizations are out there lobbying for media coverage, and one earnest, middle-aged woman sending out invitations—even if they do have RSVP on them—doesn't stand a chance. Goodwill can only go so far. If you want a job professionally done, you have to pay a professional to do it.

Local newspaper photographers, as a breed, are not the subtlest of people, and what the one from the *Great Wensham Observer* was really after was a bit of cleavage. He managed to get a meager ration from Tottie Roundwood, lolling lasciviously on Sir Toby Belch's lap. He tried to persuade Talya Northcott to take up a provocative pose, but was quickly deterred by a righteous blast of political correctness. And he was disappointed to find Sally Luther (whose tits had once been quite famous) doubleted up to the neck in her male Cesario rather than her female Viola costume. Her face was framed by a pageboy-cut blond wig, identical to the one Russ Lavery would wear as her twin, Sebastian.

Gavin Scholes fussed around, objecting to details

such as the fact that in the play Fabian would never put his arms round Viola—least of all when she was dressed as a man—but he was ignored. The photographer just pressed on, taking his clichéd shots against the garden features and constantly looking at his watch. He wasn't an exemplar of the Cecil Beaton school of photography—he had more the railway station-booth approach. After about five minutes he shoved his camera back in its bag, pulled out an old envelope on which he scribbled down the cast's names—in a way that didn't inspire confidence he'd got them right—and hurried off to do the Wildfowl Week.

Sally Luther had been a bit tight-lipped about the perfunctory nature of the photo call, but then she had had plenty of better-orchestrated ones to compare it with. Charles Paris was unworried. In his new, benign mood, little worried him, and he quite enjoyed being photographed—even for the *Great Wensham Observer*. He felt secure in his costume, secure in his role, secure in his life.

And after the photographs would come the interviews. Yes, he quite relished the idea of expatiating on his past career and his current interpretation of Sir Toby Belch. Local newspapers, he knew, were always desperate to fill space, so he'd be allowed to spread himself. It was about time Charles Paris gave an in-depth interview.

When they went back into the dining hall, he was waylaid by the earnest young girl with the cassette recorder even before he had time to get a drink. "Tell me, Mr. Parrish,'' she asked, ''what's it like working with Russ Lavery?''

THE PRESS didn't stay long. They did routine interviews with Sally Luther and left, saying they'd got all the biographical information they needed on file or they'd get it from the press release.

Vasile Bogdan glowered even more darkly at their ignoring him, and Talya Northcott looked pretty miffed. She had quite fancied the idea of a nice personality interview with her for Mummy's scrapbook.

Tottie Roundwood, of a naturally equable disposition and someone who'd been around the business a long time, was unflustered by the disregard. And Charles Paris couldn't complain about lack of attention—even if his whole interview had been about working with Dr. Mick Hobson of *Air-Sea Rescue.*

The two reporters departed having drunk only one glass of mineral water. The girl had that. The man had nothing. The accountable nineties were really wreaking havoc with journalistic stereotypes. Still, that does leave an awful lot of wine to be consumed by those who've remained, thought Charles comfortably.

Not many did remain, apart from the *Twelfth Night* representatives. For form's sake, Gavin had staged a weary little tantrum to Julian Roxborough-Smith about the lack of press presence and the waste of a day's rehearsal; and then the Festival's artistic director had gone off, scolding a still-apologetic Pauline Monkton for the lack of response to her invitations. ''But they did all have RSVP on them,'' she was heard to wail as they left the dining room.

The locals who stayed to drink with the *Twelfth Night* company were all involved in the Festival, and the majority of them were volunteers. Apart from Julian Roxborough-Smith, the Society only had one paid employee, who, in common with most people working in ''the arts,'' was paid a pittance for her services. She was the administrator, Moira Handley, the one whose cough had saved her boss from a gaffe over the Festival's sponsorship.

Moira was fortyish, thin with short, dark hair. She wore black jeans, a sloppy red jumper, and that expression of sardonic long-suffering that Charles had seen on the faces of so many stage managers over the years. It said, ''What you're asking for is totally impossible, but don't worry, I'll do it somehow.'' It was a coping expression.

Charles had always found that look reassuring, because of the rock-solid competence it implied. Not only that, he'd also always found it rather sexy. His career had encompassed some very pleasant interludes with stage managers. Their attitude to sex he'd found equally practical; and they didn't cling.

As he talked to her, Charles realized he could quite fancy Moira Handley. Or, that is to say, were he not now totally fulfilled in his relationship with Frances, he could have quite fancied Moira Handley. She wasn't wearing a wedding ring, he noticed.

Moira was talking about her boss. ''You won't see much of Julian once the Festival's up and running. I mean, he puts in an appearance today...he'll be there at your first night, I'm sure, pressing the flesh of the sponsors, but that's about it.''

"So he won't interfere artistically with the production?''

"Good heavens, no. He reckons the Shakespeare runs itself. His background's music, anyway.''

"Oh?''

"Used to be a mildly successful baritone. Was shrewd enough to move towards management before the voice went.''

"And what does he do when he's not directing festivals?''

"Not a lot. Pretty full-time job he's got doing the two of them, anyway.'' Charles looked at her quizzically. "Julian also runs the Barmington Festival—or should I say has another bunch of volunteers in Barmington who run the Barmington Festival for him.''

"I don't detect a note of criticism in your voice, do I?'' Charles asked archly.

"Good heavens, no. Julian Roxborough-Smith's very highly thought of in the arts world. On lots of advisory panels, you know, that sort of thing. No, he is reckoned to be wonderful—a perfect, cultured human being—by everyone...who hasn't worked with him.''

Charles wondered if it was the drink that was making the administrator indiscreet, but decided not. Moira Handley, he felt instinctively, was one of those people who were totally honest. She wouldn't edit her views on Julian Roxborough-Smith according to the company she was in; she'd say them to his face if he was incautious enough to ask for them.

"What makes him so difficult to work for?"

Moira puffed out her cheeks in a kind of "Take your pick" expression. "Well, in common with a lot of people who run arts festivals, he has a total inability to delegate. Julian will apportion work to others to make more time for himself, and then waste the time he's gained by looming over the shoulder of the person he's appointed to do the job. He will agree to binding decisions made in committee one day, and take the exact opposite course the next. He will independently commit the Festival to undertakings for which he has neither the mandate nor the budget. He's an autocrat who's big on the notion—though not the practice—of consultation."

Charles shrugged. "There are a lot of people in the theatre who're totally impossible to work with. Doesn't stop them being very successful."

"I know."

"Something about channeling all that energy."

Moira shook her head ruefully. "Doesn't hold up with Julian. He is the possessor of a very small amount of energy, which he husbands very carefully. In fact, Julian is basically extremely lazy. Divides his time between booking artistes who've appeared at the Great Wensham Festival for the Barmington Festival and artistes who've appeared at the Barmington Festival for the Great Wensham Festival."

"But *somebody* must get the festivals happening."

"Oh, yes, somebody does." She gave Charles a

cool, appraising grin. "But that somebody isn't Julian Roxborough-Smith."

Charles chuckled. "Well, from the tone of what you've said, I wouldn't imagine you'll be working for him a lot longer. Is this the first time you've done the Great Wensham Festival?"

Moira looked shocked. "Good heavens, no. I've been working with Julian for the past sixteen years."

"HELLO. I'm Carole Whittaker from HAN."

"Ah," said Charles, taking the thin hand the girl thrust toward him. She had, he noticed, an unnervingly offset, hennaed hairstyle—clearly expensively sculpted—and small, black-rimmed granny glasses. "I'm sorry—what's HAN?"

"Hertfordshire Arts Network."

"Oh, yes, Julian said you're one of the sponsors—right?"

"Not exactly. HAN's a body whose remit is to provide seed-corn funding which can enable and empower companies to input adequate community outreach and attain quality feedback in an arts context."

"Ah. Right."

It was Charles Paris's first encounter with artspeak.

BECAUSE THE TRAINS from Great Wensham back into London were frequent, and because the day's rehearsal schedule was shot to pieces anyway, there didn't seem much point in the members of the *Twelfth Night* company's stopping drinking. They deserved it. They'd been dragged all the way out to Hertfordshire for nothing; they might as well get some benefit from the day. And, after all, the booze was free.

Only Sally Luther, rigidly disciplining her career back on course, stayed with the mineral water.

The others—even Vasile's glowering could evidently be converted into smiles by sufficient alcohol—just got gigglier and gigglier. Charles was quite relieved John B. Murgatroyd wasn't there. The level of giggliness might then have become unacceptable.

Not that there was anyone left except the catering staff to find anything unacceptable. Moira and the other Great Wensham Festival Society representatives had long gone back to their offices, leaving the theatricals to get more and more boisterous.

Even Tottie Roundwood came out of her shell for once, the wine making her as raucous offstage as her Maria was on. In the illogic of alcohol, it suddenly seemed essential for her to convert everyone present to vegetarianism. Immediate support arrived from Talya Northcott, who said she'd been vegetarian since she'd started drama school, "and I've persuaded Mummy to give up meat too."

"Charles," Tottie demanded, "do you eat meat?"

"Guilty as charged," he replied. "But I do eat vegetables too."

"Do you? Good." She spread a broad gesture over the Chailey Ferrars catering. "You'd eat the vegetable stuff in that lot?"

"If it was something I liked, yes."

Talya Northcott snatched up a plate of mushroom tartlets. "Would you eat one of these?"

"I would, if I were hungry. I'm not hungry at the moment."

"Go on!" She thrust the plate up under his nose.

"What's going on over here?" Gavin Scholes, also in bonhomous mood, ambled toward them.

"Go on, eat it, Charles!"

He grinned, shaking his head away from the proferred delicacy. "Tottie and Talya are on a crusade, trying to persuade me to take up vegetarianism."

"Oh, God, why?"

"The more relevant question is, why not?" Tottie Roundwood countered. "Why aren't you a vegetarian, Gavin?"

"Because I like meat! I actually like the taste of bloody meat!"

"What about cooked meat?" asked Charles facetiously.

"Any meat. I'm a meat-eater. I'm a carnivore." Gavin's voice wobbled over the word. He was actually quite pissed. Maybe relief from the tensions of rehearsal made him more susceptible.

"But you like vegetables too," Tottie persisted.

"Yes, I like vegetables," Gavin agreed, *"in their place."* He paused, then giggled. "And their *place* is beside a dirty great big slab of meat!"

"No, come on, you taste this." Tottie Roundwood picked up one of the mushroom tartlets.

"Yes," Talya urged. "Go on."

"This is purely vegetable and yet the taste is a hundred percent more subtle than any meat you're ever going to find." Tottie Roundwood pressed the tartlet toward the director's mouth. "Go on, eat it."

"I'm too full," said Gavin. "Too full. There's so much meat in my stomach that there's not *mush room* for anything else."

This ancient pun made him laugh even more loudly—yes, he really was pissed—and Tottie took the invitation of his open mouth to cram in the mushroom tartlet. Talya Northcott giggled—she was quite pissed too. Gavin spluttered for a moment, but swallowed the delicacy down.

"Well, what do you think?" demanded Tottie. "What do you think of the taste?"

"I think it"—there was a silence before Gavin Scholes bawled out—"needs a bit more meat with it!"

The alcohol endowed this sally too with infinite wit, and they all giggled even louder. It was then that the Chailey Ferrars catering staff decided they had had enough. Discreetly, they started tidying up and edging their guests toward the door.

Charles dozed on the train back to London. At St. Pancras, since he seemed to have revived a taste for the stuff, he downed a couple of large Bell's. That evening he fell asleep halfway through the meal that Frances served him in front of the television.

So he didn't see the pursed expression on his wife's face as she closed the sitting-room door and went alone to her bed.

CHARLES PARIS had a wretched headache the next morning when he arrived at the rehearsal room to the news that Gavin Scholes had been taken ill with severe abdominal pains.

FOUR

"HE'S ALWAYS HAD problems with his digestion," said Charles. "One of those nervy types for whom everything goes to the stomach. Some people react to stress by getting depressed, some by getting migraines—"

"And some by getting drunk," John B. Murgatroyd interrupted. "Same again?"

"Well, shouldn't really."

Charles glanced at his watch, but John B. had already whipped up the two pint glasses and was on his way to the bar, throwing one of Sir Toby Belch's lines over his shoulder as he went. "'O knight! thou lackest a cup of canary: when did I see thee so put down?'"

What the hell, thought Charles. Couple of lunchtime drinks aren't going to hurt. We're not doing any proper rehearsal today, anyway. The assistant director, who had taken over in Gavin Scholes's absence, was an uncharismatic youth whose approach to the cast was too tentative to command respect. Asphodel Productions hadn't yet told him whether he'd be taking over permanently as director of *Twelfth Night,* but his unassertive manner suggested he thought this was unlikely. And the more he thought it was unlikely, the more unlikely it became.

Anyway, Charles reassured himself, he and John B.

weren't the only ones who'd defected to the pub. Across the bar sat Sally Luther, together with Chad Pearson, the chubby West Indian who was playing Feste (which was about as controversial as Gavin Scholes's casting was ever likely to get). Also present were Sally's in-house fan club. These were the two youngest members of the company, who were both fresh out of the same drama school (another testament to Gavin's lack of adventure). One was Talya North-cott and the other an assistant stage manager/walk-on, who delighted in the name of Benzo Ritter.

It certainly wasn't what he was born with—in fact, Talya thought he'd said it was a nickname from school. He must've chosen to use it either because there already was an Equity member with his given name, or—more likely—because he thought it sounded a better name with which to launch a theatrical career.

If that was the reason, Charles didn't share the opinion; but he knew young actors had always been prone to exotic excess, building fantasies of their stage names glowing above the titles of plays and television series. It was a harmless exercise of the imagination, and one with which even a cynical old ham such as Charles Paris could still empathize.

For a young actor, the possibilities of a showbiz career appear infinite. Each job, however minor, is the next rung on the inevitable climb to becoming the new Olivier. They all know they're going to get to the top; it's simply a question of how long it's going to take.

Charles, in whose battered heart such fatuous ambitions could still be ignited by a sudden phone call or a good rehearsal, couldn't yet judge whether Benzo Ritter had the talent to realize his dreams. As well as being an ASM, the young actor had been cast as one of the officers who arrest Antonio in act 3, scene 4. He was the Second Officer, which was unfortunate for him, because the First Officer has the lion's share of the lines.

All Benzo had to say was, "Antonio, I arrest thee at the suit of Count Orsino," "Come away, sir," and "Come, sir, I pray you go." On their second appearance in act 5, scene 1, the First Officer is the only one who speaks. So, the only opinion Charles had formed was that Benzo Ritter, in common with most young actors in their first parts, had a tendency to make too much of his minimal contribution to the play.

There was no immediate glow of talent, such as that Russ Lavery had shown in his first job, Gavin Scholes's *Macbeth* at Warminster. Still, learning to act is a long process, there's a lot of luck involved, and Benzo Ritter might yet make it to the top of the profession.

Certainly he and Talya Northcott seemed willing to learn. They watched rehearsals avidly, particularly when their idol, Sally Luther, was involved. Sally took their devotion in good part; it seemed to amuse her rather than anything else.

The conversation at the other table appeared animated, though, Charles noticed with a small twinge of guilt, they were all on the mineral water. The twinge lasted the microsecond until John B. Murgatroyd returned from the bar.

"Sorry, they were fresh out of canary," he announced, putting the two full pint glasses down on the table. "Had to make do with bitter."

"Oh, well. Needs must when the devil drives." Charles Paris took a long swallow. Nice stuff, beer. Three pints'd have him peeing all afternoon, but it was nice stuff.

"Irritable bowel syndrome," he announced.

John B. Murgatroyd cocked a quizzical eyebrow. "You too, mate?"

"No, irritable bowel syndrome is what Gavin was told he'd got last time he went to the doctor about it. He's always been a bit of a hypochondriac, and he seemed quite relieved to actually have a name given to his condition."

"So he's got an irritable bowel, has he?"

"I guess so."

"I must introduce it to my grumbling appendix," said John B. "I'm sure they could have a wonderful time moaning away at each other."

Charles gave the joke a token chuckle, then looked pensive. "Mind you, what Gavin's got now sounds a bit more serious than just irritable bowel. I mean, that wouldn't put him right out of the production, would it?"

"I suppose it depends how irritable it is. If his bowel's absolutely bloody furious, then I'd imagine—"

Charles shook his head. "Wouldn't be hospitalized with just that. Wouldn't be all this talk of 'tests.' No, I reckon it sounds a bit nasty." He took another substantial swig of beer. "Oh, well, no doubt we'll get more details in time."

His tone was rueful. The news of Gavin's illness had cast a shadow, threatening his uncharacteristically upbeat mood of recent weeks. Maybe things have been going too well, he thought gloomily, can't last.

"Come on, Charles, perk up." John B. quoted Sir Toby again. "'I'm sure care's an enemy to life.'"

"Yes, I'm sure it is too."

The other *Twelfth Night* party was moving across to the door. Benzo Ritter, Charles noticed, glowed with excitement. Was it just the thrill of being in a professional production, or had it something to do with being with the undoubtedly dishy Sally Luther?

"You two coming?" asked Chad Pearson in his lilting Caribbean tones.

"In a minute." Charles raised his glass. "Just finish this."

"See you then." Charles watched Chad and the others out of the pub, then turned back to confront an exaggerated expression of reproach on John B. Murgatroyd's face. "What's up?"

"You just don't care, do you?" said John B. in a voice of camp petulance. "I just give, give, give, all the time, and you just take, take, take."

Charles grinned, wondering what this latest performance was in aid of.

"I mean, I don't ask a lot, Charles, but I would have thought there are certain basic reciprocal rules of friendship that just *ought* to be observed." John B.

Murgatroyd flicked back a piqued eyebrow and gave a little snort of martyrdom.

"What are you on about, you idiot?"

"Well...I'd have thought it was obvious. We came into this bar—what, an hour ago?—and I bought us two drinks. When we'd drunk those, *you* went and bought us two more. When we'd drunk those, *I* went and bought two more. And now..." John B. drained his beer glass and turned to his friend with a smug grin. "Your round, I think, Charles?"

"But we shouldn't..." All too easily, Charles Paris caved in. "Same again?"

"You bet."

CHARLES HAD a headache again the next morning. The trouble was, once he started drinking, he did have a tendency to continue. Stupid habit, he could recognize that. And it was already proving destructive. Frances had been a little less than forthcoming at breakfast. Mustn't slip back into the old ways, he told himself. What he'd got going with his wife was far too important to be jeopardized by a little carelessness on his part. Pull yourself together, Charles.

The assistant director was even less assertive that morning. Something in the doomy way he put the cast through their paces suggested he now definitely knew he wasn't going to take over the production on a permanent basis.

They were doing act 5, the final scene, for which Gavin Scholes had done a rough blocking the previous week. The action was complicated, with all the principal characters—except Maria—coming in in turn to tie up the various threads of plot. As a result there was a lot of hanging around for everyone.

Charles himself didn't have much to do. Sir Toby Belch's only contribution to act 5 is to be led in, drunk and bruised, by Feste, to say a few bad-tempered, truculent lines, and be led off again. In Charles's current state, little acting was required.

While the rest of the cast were reminded of their moves, he sat slumped on a chair, head aching too much even to contemplate the *Times* crossword. Tottie Roundwood sat beside him, but mercifully did not seem in a mood to chat. Charles's mind alternated wearily between two familiar poles—swearing he'd never touch another drop of alcohol, and looking forward to the first life-restoring drink at lunchtime.

John B. Murgatroyd seemed unaffected by the excesses of the day before. Indeed, he was infuriatingly bouncy and on top. He'd probably been sensible and not continued drinking into the evening. If only Charles could learn to do that...

The atmosphere in the rehearsal room was bad, even for those who weren't hungover. Though the *Twelfth Night* company had all bitched behind Gavin Scholes's back about his lack of imagination, they had found him an unchallenging, reassuring presence. They liked the way he gave them only minimal notes on interpretation; few actors object to being allowed to play parts as they want to play them. And while he was around, they'd all shared the communal warmth of a show that felt good, a production that was going to work.

Without him they were bereft, and their mood was further weakened by the faltering suggestions of the assistant director. Tensions came to the surface.

The one in whom they were most evident was Russ Lavery. Having taken the decision to "get back to his theatrical roots" in the surprisingly minor role of Sebastian, he had been extremely obedient and self-effacing under Gavin's direction. Except for the blowup over attendance at the press conference, he had demonstrated none of the starry behavior that might be expected from someone so used to being the center of attention.

With Gavin removed, however, Russ Lavery became a very different creature. He seemed wound-up, impatient when the assistant director spent time with other actors. Suddenly he seemed to think that Sebastian was the only person in the play who mattered. He injected into the rehearsal room that unease that only a discontented star can bring. Even when he was sitting silently away from the action, no one could be unaware of his seething resentment.

The awareness was greatest in the assistant director, who looked frankly terrified and winced visibly, anticipating an outburst, every time Russ Lavery shifted in his chair.

Charles Paris was reminded of a story—maybe apocryphal, maybe not—of the great Edith Evans. One day at rehearsal she decided that the director had been taking too much interest in a speech delivered by one of her supporting actors, so swanned up to him and demanded, "And what am I meant to do in this long pause while he's talking?"

The cast member of whom Russ Lavery seemed most jealous was Sally Luther. Every time the assistant director gave a note for Viola, the star of *Air-Sea Rescue* sighed with exasperation, as if commenting on the incompetence of someone who needed so much guidance. This was completely unfair. It was early days of rehearsal, the notes Sally was given were largely technical ones relating to movement or position, but Russ still implied that she was at fault.

Charles suspected a hidden agenda in all this. Maybe Russ Lavery and Sally Luther had known each other before. Maybe it was some resentment born of television, the rising star not liking to be yoked in with the forgotten one. Perhaps Sally Luther's presence in the company was too vivid a reminder of the fickle nature of the medium that had puffed Russ Lavery up so high.

Whatever the cause of the friction, it was strange that it had never manifested itself before.

The climax of bad feeling came at the moment when Viola—dressed in male clothes as Cesario—and Sebastian come face-to-face and catalog the coincidences of their lives.

"'My father had a mole upon his brow,'" said Sally Luther.

"'And so had mine,'" Russ Lavery agreed.

"'And died that day when Viola from her birth had numbered thirteen years.'"

Sally stopped. "Do you think she should be sad here?"

"Sad?" echoed the assistant director uneasily.

"Yes, I mean sad because she's remembering her father, who she loved and—"

"Oh, for Christ's sake!" Russ Lavery erupted. "She's not bothered about her father now! She's over the moon because she thought Sebastian was dead and she's found him alive!"

"But has she actually realized Sebastian's alive yet? Is she actually sure that—"

"Sally, of course she's bloody sure! You have to remember—Viola's not as stupid as you are. You've got to play her intelligent, for God's sake. Tricky for you perhaps, but maybe it'll help if you think of it as a character part!"

The whole rehearsal room reeled at the sheer rudeness of Russ's attack. The assistant director, the one who should have defused the atmosphere, stood fidgeting awkwardly. But one voice did leap to Sally Luther's defense. Surprisingly, it came from the Second Officer.

"Russ, that was an unforgivable thing to say. Apologize at once."

"What!" The television star rounded on Benzo Ritter. "And just who the hell do you think you are, to speak to me like that?"

The boy stood his ground. "And just who the hell do you think you are, to speak to Sally like that?"

"I am an experienced actor with a lot of good work

under his belt—not some incompetent teenager with no talent and a silly name!''

''Now, listen, Russ, don't you dare—''

''Stop it! Stop it!'' came another voice as the two squared up to each other. ''Let's just get on with the rehearsal, shall we?''

It was Sally herself. She was a pragmatist. Russ Lavery had been extremely offensive to her, but Sally saw that as his problem rather than hers. Certainly nothing to stop the rehearsal for.

Benzo Ritter and his opponent edged away from each other. With bad grace, Russ Lavery resumed his rehearsal position. The younger actor gazed hopefully at Sally Luther, perhaps seeking some accolade for his intervention, but she didn't look at him, just resumed her place facing Sebastian. She was not going to let temperament and bad manners from other members of the company get in the way of her performance.

''Hm,'' murmured Tottie Roundwood to Charles Paris. ''That young man may not be going the best way to further his theatrical career.''

''How do you mean?''

''Russ Lavery thinks of himself as very important…because of the television and everything. Trouble is, he probably *is* quite important—now Gavin's not there to rein him in a bit.'' She shook her head. ''No, I would say this show is in serious need of a director.''

Charles nodded. ''Wonder who it'll be…not him, will it?'' He nodded toward the assistant director, who stood awkwardly chewing his fingers and looking down at his copy of *Twelfth Night.*

"No way." Tottie Roundwood grinned confidently. "Don't worry. I'm sure Asphodel will get someone *good.*"

The rehearsal dragged on through its uninspiring course. There were no more open confrontations, though an undercurrent of resentment remained. Gavin Scholes's patterns of movement and tableaux were more or less accurately re-created, and at last the stage area was emptied of all characters except for Feste, the Clown.

Chad Pearson moved forward to center stage, sat down cross-legged, and began to sing.

When that I was and a little tiny boy,
  With hey, ho, the wind and the rain,
A foolish thing was but a toy,
  For the rain it raineth every day....

As he sang through to the end of the song, the room stilled. He had a beautiful light voice, and the tune either was or sounded a traditional English one. Singing, Chad Pearson ceased to be a short, tubby West Indian and became a natural part of Shakespeare's world; there seemed no incongruity at that moment about the presence of a black Feste at the Illyrian court. It was not just voguish casting against ethnic stereotype. He felt right in the part, and the song was the day's only moment of genuine theatre.

The cast left for lunch in slightly improved spirits.

THE "GO ON, you'll feel better if you have a drink"
voice in Charles's head beat the "I'm never going to
touch another drop of alcohol" one. Again. But he and
John B. Murgatroyd did only have a couple of pints
each, so they felt relatively virtuous.

In fact their sense of virtue was a little specious.
They had been contemplating a third pint, but just at
that moment Benzo Ritter, in his assistant stage manager role, appeared in the pub, ordering everyone back
to the rehearsal room. A representative of Asphodel
Productions had just arrived. With an announcement
to make.

"...AND I'M AFRAID the hospital can't see any prospect
of Gavin returning to work in the short term. I'm sure
he will make a complete recovery, but it's going to
take time.

"And time, with just three weeks till this production
starts a four-month touring program, is something we
don't have a lot of."

The man from Asphodel Productions, whose name
Charles hadn't caught, wore a dark suit and looked
more like an accountant or a lawyer than an impre-
sario. Probably he was an accountant or a lawyer.
They seemed to be running most areas of show business nowadays.

Charles felt a twinge of regret for the more

colorful characters he had worked for in the past. His memory instantly summoned up a gallery of producers, agents, managers, and fixers. A rogues' gallery, it had to be said. Many of them had fabricated completely indefensible contracts. Many had inexplicably disappeared just when the company was due to be paid. Many had screwed everyone they worked with—particularly the leading ladies. But Charles Paris couldn't help feeling nostalgic for the dead, gone days.

Probably, his cynicism told him, nothing had changed that much, anyway. Nowadays the producers wore suits and had their deals checked and authenticated by lawyers, but they were still out for as much as they could get. Show business management, like horse racing and boxing, has always attracted its share of shady characters—not to say crooks.

"So," the Asphodel Productions man went on, "we need to appoint a director as soon as possible." He looked across at the assistant director, who hung his head in a rather shamefaced way. "And while we very much appreciate the way you've held the fort, Nick, for the last couple of days…as you know, we need to look for someone with a bit more experience for a production of this scale. Don't worry, what you've done for us has not gone unnoticed and your day will definitely come."

I doubt it, thought Charles, realizing that it was the first time he'd been aware the assistant director's name was Nick. The boy had so little charisma that even his name didn't register. But the quiet way in which he took the news of his demotion showed he had been told of it beforehand.

"We have been very fortunate, however," the Asphodel executive continued, "very, very fortunate...to secure the services of someone we've been keen to work with for a long time...one of the most dynamic and exciting new directors currently working in the British theatre..."

Oh, dear, thought Charles Paris, I don't like the sound of this.

"I say working in the British theatre, but in fact a lot of his work has been abroad and he's only recently come to this country. But I'm sure all of you who know how much of a stir his vivid and radical reinterpretation of *She Stoops to Conquer* at the Old Vic caused...will not need me to tell you his name."

There was a murmur of stunned appreciation from the cast, though Charles wanted to say, "I need you to. Please, please. I don't know who you're talking about."

The information came, anyway. "I'm referring of course to Alexandru Radulescu. He had been due to return to Romania shortly, but when he heard of our problems, he very graciously deferred his plans. Alexandru will be starting work with you tomorrow morning, and I think it's extremely exciting news."

From the expressions around the room, a lot of

the cast shared this opinion. In particular, Russ Lavery, Vasile Bogdan, and Tottie Roundwood were positively ecstatic at the news. The name had impressed Talya Northcott and Benzo Ritter too. Sally Luther, Charles noticed, looked considerably less keen.

"So, though of course we at Asphodel are very sorry about Gavin Scholes's illness, I feel that this particular ill wind is going to blow us all a great deal of good. Alexandru Radulescu is the sort of director whose productions really put a company on the map. And, when I talked to him about the project this morning, he was already full of ideas. He's as excited about the whole thing as all of us at Asphodel are. He says he's been dying to get his hands on Shakespeare for years."

Oh, no, Charles Paris inwardly groaned. Anything but that.

FIVE

"THAT'S NOT THE POINT, Charles."

"But I'd have thought—"

"No," Frances steamrollered on. "I am not criticizing you for coming back late. You're a grown man, for God's sake. It's up to you how you spend your time, who you drink with—that's your business. What I am objecting to is you coming back late to *my* flat."

"If you're trying to get rid of me..."

"I am not trying to get rid of you. All I'm saying is that if you're going to be staying here with me"—Charles noticed that she hadn't said "*living* here with me"—"then we have to have certain ground rules. It's just a matter of information. All I'm asking is that you let me know when you're likely to be in, *if* you're likely to be in. All you have to do is pick up a phone."

Frances caught the expression in Charles's eye and pursed her lips ruefully. "Yes, yes, yes. I know I'm sounding just like a nagging wife, but I'm afraid if we put ourselves back into a cohabiting situation, then I'm going to come back with all the things wives usually nag about. It's not what I want, Charles. I don't want to be forced into a stereotype."

"No, no, I can see that."

"Look, my life is actually very well sorted at the

moment. I've got used to living on my own. I've actually got quite efficient at it. And I don't want to be taken back to square one."

"I don't want to take you back to square one. Honestly, Frances." He took her hand, comforted by the familiar ridge of the old kitchen-knife scar. "I'm thinking in terms of square five at least. Maybe even square six..."

She shook her head wryly.

"...and then, who knows—we might find that there's a ladder on square six leading straight up to square seventy-four."

"More likely a snake to send us thumping down to square one again." But at least she smiled as she said it.

Charles tightened the pressure on her hand. "Look, Frances, I really mean what I'm saying now. This last couple of weeks has been the best thing that's happened for years. For me, nothing has ever replaced what there is between us."

"Though you've tested out a good few options on the way to that conclusion, haven't you, Charles?" said Frances with a beady look.

He shook his head in exasperation. "Yes, all right. But that's over now. That part of my life's behind me."

"Oh, yes?"

"Yes. Other women... All that other women have ever showed me is that you're the only woman who's right for me. You're what I want, Frances."

"Are you talking permanence here, Charles?"

"Yes. Well, possibly... Maybe... I mean, obviously not in the short term."

"Oh, no. Obviously not."

"Nothing's going to happen quickly. I just feel that there's such a bond between us we should test it out, see how strong it really is. Try and get back together."

Frances was silent, but her expression didn't show wholehearted conviction about what he was saying.

"Look, I know there've been times in the past when I've been inconsiderate, when I've hurt you..."

He let the pause lengthen. Then Frances said suddenly, "I'm sorry. You're not expecting me to disagree, are you?"

"No, of course I'm not." Mind you, some token contradiction wouldn't have hurt. "But this time I am really determined to make it work. We've got so much to give each other, and I think we should try to make the best of the time we have left...and make the best of that time...together."

"The trouble with actors," said Frances, removing her hand, "is that they're all full of shit...and full of half-remembered lines from shows they've been in. Go on, tell me. Where did that last line you said come from?"

Charles looked shamefaced. "Comedy called *The Twang of a Heartstring*. Hornchurch in the early seventies. Can still remember quite a lot of the lines from it, actually."

He could also still remember the review that the *Hornchurch Herald* had given his performance: "If Charles Paris was meant to be Love's Young Dream, it suggested Love had been eating rather too much toasted cheese before going to bed.''

He took her hand again. ''All right, what I said was garbage, but the intention wasn't garbage. I'm really determined to make this work, Frances.''

Her face was still a conviction-free zone. ''Even if it means making concessions?''

''Of course.''

''Living by the rules I dictate?''

''Sure.''

''Allowing me to continue having a life of my own? To have parts of my life that are not your business?''

''Yes, all that.''

''Mm.'' Frances was pensive for a moment, then came to a decision. ''Okay, let's give it a whirl.''

''Great.'' Charles squeezed her hand.

''Right,'' she went on briskly. ''Tonight I don't want you here.''

''Oh?''

''Till after midnight. You can come back then.''

''Thank you.'' A silence. ''May I ask...?''

''I thought you'd just agreed to allow me to have parts of my life that're not your business.''

''Well, yes, but—''

''All right then. I've got a friend coming round.''

''Oh. Anyone I know?''

''No, Charles. Nobody you know.''

AFTER FRANCES HAD GONE to school, Charles was left with a little niggle of disquiet. Not jealousy, surely? No, she'd just been playing a game with him. It was a small revenge for her. *You* come back late and pissed, *I*'ll be mysterious about some unnamed friend I've got. Tit for tat.

What worried him more was that the niggle might presage a shift in his mood. He'd been so positive the last few weeks. Everything had been going so well. Now suddenly there was the professional threat of the unknown in the form of Alexandru Radulescu, and privately, a new edginess in his relationship with Frances.

Oh, well, if I'm going to go down, I may as well go down properly. To compound his mood, he rang his agent, Maurice Skellern.

''Yes, I had heard. I do keep my ear to the ground on my clients' behalf, you know, Charles.'' Maurice's voice was full of reproach at the idea that he wasn't aware of *Twelfth Night*'s change of director.

''And do you know anything about him?''

''Not a lot. Hasn't been in this country long. Comes from Bulgaria, doesn't he?''

''Romania.''

''Same difference. And he's done a couple of productions over here that've got the chattering classes very excited. Gets all those reviews which use words like *radical and mold-breaking*.''

''Yes,'' said Charles gloomily. ''And 'Radulescu's production made one feel one was seeing an entirely different play.'''

''That's right. Now what paper was that in?''

''I just made it up.''

"Really? I could have sworn I've read it somewhere quite recently."

"You probably have." Charles groaned. Oh, well, might as well lower his mood even further. "Anything on the horizon...you know, workwise?"

The reproach in Maurice Skellern's voice was now ladled on with a trowel. "Greedy, Charles, greedy. Let me get my breath back. After all, I've secured you a four-month contract with Asphodel."

"Gavin Scholes rang me direct and offered me that, Maurice. *I* told *you* about it."

"Ah, maybe, but I was the one who sorted out the deal."

"You accepted the first offer they made."

"Charles, Charles, when will you realize? What I do is a very finely tuned business. Involves a lot of very delicate decisions. Sometimes you have to push like mad, scrabble for more and more money from them. Other times you have to be subtle—sit back, hold your fire, live to fight another day."

"Funny it's always other clients you do the scrabbling for. When it comes to me, on the other hand, you always seem to be holding your fire."

"Charles, that's very cruel. If I didn't know you so well, I'd find that extremely hurtful. You've no idea how much I do behind the scenes on your behalf."

"I've a nasty feeling I have, Maurice."

"Charles, trust me..." How many times must Maurice have said that over the years. And every time Charles'd heard the words, they had prompted the identical reaction: "I assume you're joking." And yet, in all their long association, he'd never once vocalized the thought.

"If I didn't know what I was doing," Maurice went on, "ask yourself—would you still be one of my clients after all these years?"

Yes, thought Charles Paris, savage with self-contempt, *I* would.

"'APPROACH, SIR ANDREW: not to be abed after midnight is to be up betimes; and *diluculo surgere*, thou knowest—'"

"'Nay, by my troth, I know not; but I know that to be up late is to be up late.'"

"'A false conclusion!'" Charles bellowed, wishing he hadn't been up quite so late the night before. It had been stupid to engage Frances in conversation about how she'd spent her evening. The sensible course would have been to take the hint of her closed bedroom door and go off to sleep in the spare room. And that's what he would have done if he hadn't drunk so much. Still, he told himself with the wounded logic of someone who knows he's in the wrong, it was her fault. If she turfs me out and I'm not allowed back in till after midnight, how does she imagine I'm going to spend the evening?

"'I hate it as an unfilled can,'" Charles continued, thinking how much he'd welcome a filled can to irrigate his desiccated brain. He felt a bit gutty too; that really meant he'd had too much the night before. "'To be up after midnight and to go to bed then, is early; so that to go to bed after midnight is to go to bed betimes. Does not our life consist of the four elements?'"

"'Faith, so they say,'" John B. Murgatroyd's Sir Andrew Aguecheek weedily agreed, "'but, I think, it rather consists of eating and drinking.'"

And sex, thought Charles wistfully. He shouldn't have put his hand on Frances's shoulder the night before. He should have respected her privacy rather than trying it on. His behavior had been juvenile and crass and she'd been absolutely right to tell him to leave her alone. Oh, God... He hoped he hadn't cast a permanent blight over his prospects of making love to Frances again. Why was he capable of such total idiocy?

"'Thou art a scholar,'" Sir Toby Belch went on, "'let us therefore eat and drink. Marian, I say! a stoup of wine!'"

The assistant director stopped them there. He was still in charge of the first part of the morning's rehearsal. Alexandru Radulescu had a meeting at the National Theatre and wouldn't be with them till about twelve.

"Just like to take it from the top again," the assistant director suggested nervously.

"Anything specific wrong?" asked Charles, hoping that the hangover wasn't spoiling his performance.

"No, not really. Just need a bit more contrast between you, I think. Sir Andrew really is knackered. All he wants to do is go to bed. So we need more of Sir Toby jollying him along. Be more of a party animal, Charles."

"Right, okay." It was a good point. In fact, the

assistant director's ideas were all good; he just didn't have the personality to put them across with sufficient definition.

Even through his hangover, Charles knew that the double act with John B. was going well. They looked good together. A long, willowy Sir Andrew Aguecheek and a more substantial—thanks to the padding, Charles kept reassuring himself—Sir Toby Belch. A kind of Don Quixote and Sancho Panza in reverse. Then of course Charles would have his ruddied face, and John B. would make his as pale as milk. Yes, they'd look great.

It was so good to be working on a classic. The relationship between Sir Toby and Sir Andrew has a kind of mythic quality. The crafty drunkard and the ineffectual dupe. The parts Shakespeare wrote are so solid, almost tactile, and yet with infinite nuances to be explored. Even the lines are easy to learn because they feel so right. Charles was really going to enjoy Sir Toby Belch—or at least he was as soon as he'd got rid of his hangover. His guts felt distinctly squittery. He had a nasty feeling he was going to have to make a rush to the gents before too long.

They pressed on through act 2, scene 3. Chad Pearson joined them and his rendering of another of Feste's songs again reduced the rehearsal room to silence.

O mistress mine! where are you roaming?
O! stay and hear; your true love's coming.
   That can sing both high and low.
Trip no further, pretty sweeting;

Journeys end in lovers meeting,
Every wise man's son doth know.

They worked through to the end of the scene, though the cement-mixer rumbling of Charles's stomach was getting louder and louder. He felt sure everyone could hear it. Thank God I'm not doing a radio, he thought.

He just made it to the end. "'Come, come: I'll go burn some sack; 'tis too late to go to bed now. Come, knight; come, knight.'"

"Very nice," said the assistant director. "Very nice indeed. Erm, I'd just like to—"

"Sorry, must dash," panted Charles Paris.

It was a close call getting to the gents in time, and as he squatted back exhausted on the lavatory, he swore he'd never touch another drop of alcohol. It was insane, putting his body through this kind of punishment.

Charles was pulling up his trousers when he heard the sound of two men coming in to use the urinals. Instinctively, as everyone does in that situation, he froze, embarrassed to give away his presence in the cubicle.

The men were talking, but in a language Charles had never heard before. One of the voices was familiar, though. Yes, in spite of the words, the deep tones were recognizable as those of Vasile Bogdan.

It seemed reasonable to assume that he was talking Romanian; and that the man he was talking to was Alexandru Radulescu.

Charles couldn't be sure, but in amongst the strange words, he thought he heard the director mention Gavin Scholes. There was a sound of zipping up, then the footsteps and voices moved away.

Vasile Bogdan let out a harsh laugh as the door was opened. Then, in English, he said, ''Well, it worked, anyway, Alex. Gavin's out of the way, and you've got the job.''

SIX

"OKAY." Alexandru Radulescu moved his spread hands outward in a that's-enough-of-that gesture. "*Twelfth Night* is a play about sex."

Well, only partly, thought Charles. It's more a play about romance, romantic ideals and how they frequently mismatch with reality.

"*All* plays are about sex," the director continued in his heavily accented voice. "All life is about sex, if you like, and so of course Shakespeare, who reflected life, writes only about sex..."

Now just a minute, hang on there. In Charles's view, Shakespeare wrote about everything. That included sex, sure, but to call sex his overriding obsession seemed an unnecessarily simplistic and Freudian interpretation.

"...and nowhere is that more true than in *Twelfth Night*. When I first read the play..."

Which was probably last night, was Charles's instant reaction. He was having no difficulty being uncharitable to this small, wiry, dark-eyed Romanian. It wasn't just from suspicion raised by what he'd overheard in the gents. Alexandru Radulescu had a deliberately provocative manner. He seemed to enjoy putting people's backs up. As yet none of the company had raised any objections to what he was saying, but when that did happen, Charles felt the director would enjoy slapping them down.

"When I first read the play, I thought, 'Sex, sex, sex'—that's what's happening here. Exciting young sex with Sebastian..." He flashed a smile at Russ Lavery, who grinned back knowingly. "Sebastian and Olivia, yes, but also Sebastian and Antonio."

Charles groaned inwardly. He hated productions that imposed twentieth-century values on the society of Shakespeare's time. In the sixteenth century there had been a strong tradition of masculine friendship and loyalty. A line like Antonio's to Sebastian, "If you will not murder me for my love, let me be your servant," did not imply a full-blown homosexual affair...though Charles had a nasty feeling that's how a director like Alexandru Radulescu would interpret it—no doubt with lots of gratuitous male kissing and mime of sexual congress. The good burghers of Great Wensham weren't going to like that.

"There is also old sex—disgusting geriatric groping between Sir Toby Belch and Maria..."

Now just a minute...Charles had always thought there was something rather heartwarming in the relationship between Sir Toby and Maria. He tried to assess how old Alexandru Radulescu was. Early thirties perhaps. Certainly of the age that reckoned sex was turned off like a bath tap at the age of fifty. Huh, he's got a thing or two to learn. But that thought brought a pang of unease, reminding Charles of the previous evening's scene with Frances.

"But there is also—and most important of all—an

uncertainty about sexual identity. This is at the center of the play—Viola searching for her own sexuality by the experiment of cross-dressing..."

No, no, no, that isn't at the center of the play.

"...Orsino being brought face-to-face with his homosexuality through his infatuation with Cesario..."

No.

"...Malvolio's obsession with Olivia, which is fetishistic and can only find expression through bondage in the form of yellow cross-garters... This is what Shakespeare meant us to take from *Twelfth Night*."

No, it isn't. That's just what you want to impose on *Twelfth Night*.

"Right, so bear all this in mind as we work on the play. Sex, sex, sex." Alexandru Radulescu looked across to the assistant director. "Okay, maybe we should start."

"Yes, well, we've just rehearsed act two, scene three. Would you like us to run that, and maybe we can see places where, you know...the sexual element can be emphasized a bit?"

"What!" Alexandru Radulescu stared at the young man, appalled. "You think I am just going to pick up the leftovers of someone else's production?"

"Well, it's all been blocked...the cast know their moves and lines...I mean, we do only have three weeks before we open and—"

The director drew himself up to his full—not very great—height. "Alexandru Radulescu does not collaborate! When Alexandru Radulescu directs a production, he does it his way. And, anyway, Alexandru Radulescu does not just direct, he *reinterprets* a play.''

It'll end in tears, thought Charles Paris. It'll end in tears.

''IT COULD HAVE meant anything,'' said John B. Murgatroyd. They were sitting over drinks at the end of that day's rehearsal. John B. had a pint of bitter; Charles was on the large Bell's. For him beer spelled relaxation, and an afternoon in the company of Alexandru Radulescu had rendered him desperate for whiskey.

'''Well, it worked, anyway,''' John B. quoted again. ''Vasile probably just meant that Alexandru had cracked the British system—made himself the natural candidate to take over when Gavin got ill.''

''Equally it could have meant that their plan to *make* Gavin ill had worked.''

''Oh, for heaven's sake, Charles. You're the last person I'd have expected to be a conspiracy theorist. What, so you've also got proof that Kennedy was assassinated by Elvis Presley and Marilyn Monroe because he threatened to tell Martin Luther King about their love child—is that right? You're being paranoid.''

''Don't you think this afternoon's events justify a little paranoia?''

''Hmm...'' John B. Murgatroyd took a thoughtful swallow of his beer. ''It'll probably be all right. Look, he hasn't got time to make too many changes. I'm sure he's mostly talk—that sort always are. What we'll end up with is a straight telling of *Twelfth Night* with a couple of trendy flourishes.''

''You have the sound of someone trying very hard to convince himself—and failing. I've worked with directors like this before,'' said Charles darkly.

Various unpleasant memories bubbled to the surface of his mind. Charles Paris liked the words a playwright wrote to be the mainspring of a production; he couldn't stand directors who regarded the text as an obstacle that had to be negotiated on the way to their personal glorification.

Wincing, he remembered a production of *Richard III*, in which Richard alone remained handsome and upright, while all the other characters had been played with various disabilities. The director's point that deformity is in the eye of the beholder might have some validity in another context, but it sure as hell made nonsense of Shakespeare's play. Charles rather treasured the notice the *Wigan Gazette* had given of his one-legged Duke of Clarence (Jesus, he'd been grateful to be killed off so early—the strapping was agony): ''Charles Paris's resolute swimming in the malmsey-butt suggests a promising nautical future for him as Long John Silver.''

''Oh, God,'' Charles groaned, dragging himself out of this unwelcome recollection, ''just wait till Alexandru Radulescu starts exploring the homosexual subtext of Sir Toby Belch's relationship with Sir Andrew Aguecheek.''

''Now...the opening dumb show,'' were the first words with which the new director began the next day's rehearsal.

"But there isn't an opening dumb show," Sally Luther objected. Charles had been about to make the same point, but the coward in him was relieved she got the words in first. No point in antagonizing Alexandru unnecessarily. Charles had a gut feeling there would be plenty of other issues over which he'd really *need* to take issue with the director.

"The dumb show," said Alexandru patiently, "is a very common feature of Elizabethan theatre. Many plays were started with a dumb show, prefiguring the action to follow. Indeed, the play that Hamlet organizes to be performed before King Claudius begins with a dumb show," he concluded as if closing the argument.

Charles couldn't let that go by. "Yes, but the whole point there was that Shakespeare was deliberately presenting an archaic convention. In the same way that the First Player's language is dated and overblown, the dumb show is put there to show how unfashionable this particular troupe of traveling players are. Shakespeare always knew what he was doing. If he'd intended *Twelfth Night* to begin with a dumb show, he'd have specified a dumb show."

Charles didn't look directly at Alexandru Radulescu until the end of this speech. What he then saw was chilling. The director's black eyes were two focused pinpoints of hatred. Up until that moment their relationship had been wary but polite; now Charles felt he had made an enemy for life.

"God, that's all I need"—Alexandru spat out the words—"actors who think they're experts on Shakespeare. Listen, *I* do the thinking round this production. All that's required of you is to say the words the way I tell you to."

Charles felt as if his face had been slapped. He wanted to come back, fierce and hard, with the fact that he *did* actually know quite a lot about Shakespeare, that he'd got an Oxford degree in English to prove it, that... But he restrained himself. Time enough. No need to go out on a private offensive. Soon the rest of the company were bound to join forces in resistance to Alexandru Radulescu's fatuous innovations.

But no other members of the cast made any complaint about the idea of the dumb show. It was understandable that the youngsters such as Benzo Ritter and Talya Northcott might eagerly lap up Alexandru's suggestions, but the more mature cast members also seemed placidly content to do as they were told.

Charles often marveled at the ridiculous hoops actors will go through at the bidding of a forceful personality. *Twelfth Night*'s assistant director, whose ideas were actually rather good, could not command obedience; while Alexandru Radulescu, whose ideas were clearly crap, could lead the entire company by the nose. Sometimes Charles could empathize with Alfred Hitchcock's well-known view that "actors are cattle."

The only objection that did arise was when Alexandru Radulescu announced that for the opening of the play the stage area would be converted into a huge double bed. And the objection came, not from a cast member, but from the Asphodel representative, who had appeared to see how rehearsals were going.

"No," he said quietly but firmly.

The Romanian whirled furiously round at him. "What!"

"No room in the budget for more scenery. You've got to work with the sets as built, and with the costumes as already made."

"But how am I expected to express my vision of the play if I am saddled with unimaginative sets and traditional costumes?"

The Asphodel accountant shrugged his shoulders. "That's your problem. It was made perfectly clear in our agreement that you had to work with the existing sets and costumes. There isn't the time, apart from there not being the money, for any changes to be made there."

"But this means I will have to compromise my entire artistic perception of the play!"

The accountant shrugged again. "Well, there you go," he said coolly.

Charles Paris wished some of the cast had the nerve to take that approach to Alexandru. Because it clearly worked. Faced with a will as strong as his own, the director could only huff and puff petulantly.

"I thought you employed me because I would bring something fresh, something radical, to this production. People who employ me do so because they know they will get a play that has the Alexandru Radulescu stamp all over it!''

"I'm not interfering with your stamp," the Asphodel man replied without changing his lazy intonation. "I'm just saying that that stamp will have to appear with the existing sets and costumes. That's all. I'm not going to interfere with what you do artistically."

"But for a director like me, the art comes in the *total* look of a production. It is not just the acting—it is the movement, the music, the setting, the clothes the actors wear!"

This bluster produced no more than another shrug. "You knew the deal when you started, Alex. I'm here to control the budget, and I say you can't change the sets or the costumes."

Though the director huffed and puffed a little more, it was only token resistance. He knew he couldn't beat the moneymen. But his defeat seemed to make him determined to put his cast through more irrelevant hoops of artifice.

"Right, the dumb show," he announced again, once he'd given up grumbling as a bad job. "As I said yesterday, *Twelfth Night* is a play about sex, and I want the opening mime to reinforce this message. So it will take the form of a ritualized orgy."

Charles Paris shook his head in disbelief.

"In this way we will show the different crosscurrents of love and lust between the characters, as they come together in different combinations."

"How do you mean 'come together'?" Charles

hadn't wanted to ask the question, but couldn't help himself.

"I mean, obviously, Charles, come together as in acts of sexual congress."

"Simulated sex?"

"Exactly." With the word, Alexandru Radulescu turned a withering look on Charles. What was more worrying was that most of the cast also directed withering looks at him. Good God, they actually seemed prepared to go along with this madman's ideas.

"And," the director continued, intrigued by a new idea, "if we can't afford new costumes, then maybe we do without costumes... Yes!"

Charles's mouth dropped. "Are you suggesting we do all this simulated sex without any clothes on?"

"Of course."

"But—"

"No." Once again the authoritative monosyllable came from the Asphodel representative.

"You said you would not interfere with the artistic content of my production!"

"This is not artistic, this is financial. A *Twelfth Night* that opens with a naked orgy will be death at the box office—particularly at Great Wensham. Sorry, you can't do it."

This second rejection produced only minimal remonstrance from Alexandru. He knew when he was beaten. If things started to get really out of hand, Charles comforted himself, the Asphodel man would be the person to talk to.

The director, accepting his defeat, moved on.

"So...we will think which characters have lusts towards which others, yes?" He looked ingenuously at his cast. "Please, you tell me. I don't want to impose my ideas on you. I want you all to contribute to this production. I am a director who believes very much in ensemble thinking."

That was patent nonsense; the man was clearly an unhinged autocrat. But once again none of the cast drew attention to his hypocrisy. They seemed happy, even flattered, to be part of this illusory consultation process. A lot of them sat forward eagerly as they tried to think of potential sexual connections within *Twelfth Night.* Benzo Ritter and Talya Northcott were particularly enthused. This was what they had gone into the theatre for—the creative white heat of workshopping in the rehearsal room.

"Well, there are the obvious sexual attractions you've already mentioned, Alex," said Vasile Bogdan. His readiness to come forward suggested it was not the first time he had played this game. Vasile seemed very familiar with Alexandru's methods. Charles would have to check out whether the two Romanians had worked together before. There was something going on between them.

And he couldn't forget the words that he had overheard. In spite of John B. Murgatroyd's scorn for the idea, Charles still wondered whether Gavin Scholes's illness had been engineered. He'd have to investigate further.

"Sebastian and Olivia," Vasile went on. "Viola's

lust for Orsino. Orsino's lust for Cesario. Toby's for Maria. Malvolio's kinky obsession with Olivia..."

"And of course Orsino's obsession for Olivia at the beginning of the play," Benzo Ritter contributed. "I mean, he's totally gone on her, can't think about anything else. Waking, sleeping, his thoughts, his dreams, are full of nothing else—just Olivia."

"This is good." Alexandru Radulescu nodded enthusiastically. "And then, when he sees Viola/Cesario, it all vanishes. One obsession is instantly replaced by another. This is showing us, I think, the fickleness of obsessive love, infatuation, whatever you want to call it."

"I don't think it's saying *all* obsessive love is fickle. I mean, there are passions which endure and are rather magnificent in their—"

But Alexandru seemed unwilling to listen to more of Benzo's theories—presumably because they didn't coincide exactly with his own. "Yes, yes, yes." His eyes darted round the company. "What else have we got in the play? What other couples, what other sexual crosscurrents—eh?"

Vasile Bogdan picked up the cue again. "Well, we have Antonio's gay thing for Sebastian..."

Alexandru nodded enthusiastically. "Yes, let's keep going on this gay thing. There are other characters in the play, I am certain, who are attracted to their own sex. Who do you think? Come on, it is obvious—no?" Alexandru Radulescu looked round at the faces, exasperated by their slowness in reaching the obvious.

"Well...," said Sally Luther, "I hope you're not

suggesting that Olivia's attraction to Cesario means that deep down she's a lesbian...?''

"Why do you hope I am not suggesting this?"

"Because it's a ridiculous idea. It makes nonsense of the play's resolution when Olivia marries Sebastian."

Good for you, Sally, thought Charles. Thank God somebody's not going along with all this garbage.

The director looked piqued. "No, it does not, Sally. It makes *sense* of this. Both Olivia and Sebastian are bisexual, you understand. The two heterosexual halves of them match together and make the play's resolution, but the other halves of them are still ambiguous, unresolved. It is those sexual ambiguities which Shakespeare would have explored had he written a sequel to this play."

"What—a sort of *Thirteenth Night?*" John B. Murgatroyd suggested.

A couple of the cast snorted at this, but the expression on Alexandru Radulescu's face showed them that there weren't going to be many giggles round the production now that he was in charge. Benzo Ritter and Talya Northcott also turned reproving stares on John B. Murgatroyd; so far as they were concerned, he was being inappropriately trivial in the presence of genius.

"Please, don't let's waste our time in silliness," the director said primly.

You're a fine one to talk, thought Charles.

"So that is one gay element we have isolated, right? But there is another, very obvious one we haven't mentioned yet.'' Again Alexandru looked round the semicircle of faces. ''Come on, very obvious indeed.''

It was Tottie Roundwood who spoke finally. As she did so, she looked at the director with a respect that verged on devotion. ''Could you possibly mean...Sir Toby Belch and Sir Andrew Aguecheek?''

''Yes,'' said Alexandru Radulescu. ''Exactly.''

I don't believe this is happening, thought Charles Paris.

SEVEN

ALEXANDRU RADULESCU'S mind made a butterfly's look like a model of consistency. He behaved like a child playing in a toyshop of ideas; and perhaps, after the artistic restrictions he'd experienced in his native Romania, that was how he felt. He came into rehearsal every morning brimful of new thoughts, derived from anything he'd happened to have observed or heard or seen. He was into everything just deep enough to get the soles of his shoes wet.

For instance, he saw a mime artist busking at Covent Garden and was so impressed he brought the guy in to advise the cast on movement. Then in an Indian restaurant, by chance he heard some Eastern Muzak, which he decided had an authentic "dying fall." He immediately engaged a sitar player to do the *Twelfth Night* music. Worse than that, he got the musician to reset Feste's songs in some approximation to raga style. Chad Pearson gamely tried to ride the unfamiliar rhythms. He succeeded pretty well, but at the expense of audibility. The atmospheric, melancholy words of the songs were lost.

It was all in a way very exciting—so long as you didn't care about Shakespeare's *Twelfth Night*. Charles Paris did, and he found rehearsals agonizing. Every few minutes, it seemed, some other felicity of the play was sacrificed or obscured for a theatrical effect.

Even Charles had to admit, though, that most of the effects were striking. Alexandru Radulescu had an inspired visual sense. He created patterns of movement that were mesmerizing and dramatic.

But it was all independent of the text. He would have made as interesting a spectacle of the yellow pages as he was making of *Twelfth Night*. And Charles Paris would have preferred them to be doing the yellow pages than a text he had cherished since his schooldays.

The production's opening moments were typical of the Radulescu approach. The dumb show had survived and refined into something far less crude than first envisaged. All of the play's characters took up positions in the blackout; then, to intricate Indian rhythms, they moved like blank-faced automatons into a variety of physical combinations. Their bodies had become inhuman, like components of some intricate metal puzzle. The mime, though it still had copulatory overtones, had taken on a universal and emblematic quality. But the precision of their ensemble movement could not fail to arrest an audience's attention.

The sitar music continued as the cast froze into a tableau, facing out front, chilling the audience with the blankness of their stares. Alexandru Radulescu had wanted this moment to echo his sketchy understanding of No theatre, and only the vigilance of the Asphodel accountant had stopped him from commissioning traditional Japanese wooden masks for the entire cast.

While his fellow actors stayed immobile, Orsino then stepped forward and, with his staff, struck the stage three times (a convention borrowed from classical French theatre). He then intoned:

"'If music be the food of love, play on!'"

"On, on, on, on...," the rest of the rigid cast echoed in unison, their words tapering off to silence.

"'Give me excess of it, that, surfeiting, the appetite may sicken, and so die.'"

"Die, die, die, die...," came the dwindling echo.

"'That strain again!'"

"Again, again, again, again..."

"'It had a dying fall.'"

"Fall, fall, fall, fall..."

"'O!'"

"O, o, o, o..."

"'It came o'er my ear like the sweet sound that breathes upon a bank of violets, stealing and giving odor.'"

"Odor, odor, odor, odor..." This time the echo was as soft as breath.

"'Enough! no more.'"

Suddenly Orsino slammed his staff down onto the ground. All of the cast, except for the Duke and Curio, scattered off to the sides of the stage with the exaggerated, flickering movements of silent film.

The Indian musician let out a long lamenting twang from his sitar, and Orsino was left to continue his speech in a relatively traditional manner until Alexandru Radulescu's next theatrical sensation.

The effect was undeniably dramatic, but it had nothing to do with *Twelfth Night*.

CHARLES'S POSITION within the production was tense and difficult. Sir Toby Belch was a part he'd longed to play all his life, and he was now at the ideal...erm, maturity...to do it justice. He wouldn't get another crack at it. And he didn't want this chance buggered up by a director with no sensitivity to Shakespeare.

John B. Murgatroyd and Charles had prepared tactics over various long sessions in the pub. Basically, they both intended to play their parts as they had been playing them under Gavin Scholes's direction—and, in their view, as Shakespeare intended them to be played.

So, though they listened politely to Alexandru's suggestions, and even went through the motions of trying out his new ideas, after a couple of runs at a scene, they would revert to doing it exactly the way they had before. This did not make for a good atmosphere between the two actors and their director.

A typical moment of conflict occurred when they were rehearsing act 2, scene 3. Maria, having described her plans to dupe Malvolio, has just exited, leaving Sir Toby Belch and Sir Andrew Aguecheek united in admiration for her ingenuity. The following lines then ensue:

SIR TOBY: Good night, Penthesilea.

SIR ANDREW: Before me, she's a good wench.

SIR TOBY: She's a beagle, true-bred, and one that adores me...what o' that? (*He sighs.*)

SIR ANDREW: I was adored once too. (*He sighs also.*)
SIR TOBY: Let's to bed, knight.

Charles and John B. ran the lines as they had rehearsed them under Gavin. Alexandru Radulescu, his little body contorted into a knot of concentration, watched intently. As soon as Charles had said his "Let's to bed, knight," the director waved his hands in the air.

"Okay, okay, we stop. There is a lot here. It is a very good moment this, I think."

"Certainly is," Charles agreed. For him it was the most poignant in the play, one of those many in *Twelfth Night* where farce is suddenly shaded with melancholy. He loved the wistfulness with which John B. Murgatroyd played his "I was adored once too" and was pleased with the way he, as Sir Toby, put his arm around the ineffectual knight's shoulder and led him off. It was a brief instance of closeness between the two characters; for a second Sir Toby suspended his cynical campaign of exploitation and showed Sir Andrew a flash of human sympathy.

That was not, however, how Alexandru Radulescu saw the exchange. "Yes, very good," he repeated, looking down at his script. "As ever, Shakespeare tells us everything. It is all in the text, if only you look hard enough."

Actually, you don't have to look that hard, thought Charles. Usually the meaning in Shakespeare's lines is limpidly self-evident. Still, he was relieved that the director was finally recognizing the preeminence of the actual words.

"Now, obviously," Alexandru went on, "there are references here to the past, things that have happened before the play starts."

"Yes," Charles agreed.

"Sir Andrew talking about having been 'adored once too,'" John B. contributed.

"And," the director concluded triumphantly, "an unequivocal confirmation of the homosexual relationship between the two knights."

"What!"

"What!"

Alexandru became excited as he expounded his textual analysis. "You see, they talk about Maria. Sir Toby says she's 'one that adores me...but what of that?' In other words, he is saying, 'She fancies me, but what of that? Since I'm gay, she's wasting her time.'"

"No, he is not saying that. He's praising her."

"Praising her? How do you get that? What does he describe Maria as? A 'beagle.' This is not very flattering, I think. He is saying she is very ugly. He is saying she is a *dog*."

"*Dog* didn't have that meaning at the time Shakespeare was—"

But the director was too preoccupied even to hear counterargument. "Then Sir Andrew, all pathetic-like, reminds Sir Toby that they used to have a thing going. 'I was adored once too,' he says—doesn't he?"

"Yes, he does, but he's not referring to Sir Toby."

"Oh, no? Then why is it that Toby's next line—having been reminded that he's been neglecting Sir

Andrew emotionally—is 'Let's to bed, knight.' I mean, how overt do you want this to be? 'Let's to bed, knight'—you can't have a less ambiguous sexual proposition than that, can you?''

''Yes, of course you—''

''No, come on. What did you used to say, back in the days when you were seducing women, eh?'' Charles rather resented that implication. ''If you said 'let's to bed'—or 'let's go to bed'—it meant 'I want to screw you'—yes?''

''Look—''

''Yes or no? Did it mean 'I want to screw you' or not?''

''Well, yes, in that context it probably did, but—''

''See!'' The director spoke with the satisfaction of an ontologist into whose sitting room God has just walked.

''But, Alexandru, that is not what it means in this context. Such an idea makes nonsense of the relationship between Sir Toby and Sir Andrew. They're talking about Maria and what a great woman she is. What they're saying is in total admiration of her.''

''I think not. Look at the text, Charles. That is what you must always do when you are dealing with the work of a great genius like Shakespeare—look at the text.''

That's rich, coming from you.

''And when we look at the text, what do we see? 'Good night, Penthesilea.' Who is this Penthesilea, by the way?''

''Penthesilea,'' said Charles patiently, ''was the

queen of the Amazons. Hence, any forceful or effective woman. Sir Toby describes Maria by that name as a tribute to the skill with which she has set up the plan to fool Malvolio.''

Charles looked up, anticipating apology in the director's face, but instead saw glee. Wagging a triumphant finger, Alexandru shouted, ''You see, you see, that proves it! You've said it out of your own mouth! *Amazon* means 'any forceful or effective woman.' In other words, a dominant woman. In other words, the dominant mother whose sexuality so frightened the son that, in self-protection, he became homosexual.''

''That is psychological claptrap. Apart from anything else, it's been proved that there's no connection between—''

''What is more,'' Alexandru rolled on with satisfaction, ''*amazon* often means 'lesbian.' Hmm, I think maybe we are also getting the key to Maria's character here...''

He looked thoughtfully across to Tottie Roundwood. To Charles's annoyance, she didn't immediately point out what balls this all was. She looked pleased, even honored, to be sharing the wisdom of the guru.

''Okay.'' Alexandru clapped his hands. ''Now let's run the lines again—bearing in mind what we now know.''

''We don't know anything we didn't know before,'' Charles protested.

''No? So what are you saying? Are you saying that there is no attraction between Sir Toby Belch and Sir

Andrew Aguecheek? Are you flying in the face of William Shakespeare's text?''

"No, I am not. I am saying there is affection between them—and this is the moment in the play where that affection is most overtly expressed—but *that is all!*''

Alexandru Radulescu's mouth pursed in annoyance. "It is very difficult, you know, for a director to direct when his actors will not take direction.''

"I'll take direction as well as the next actor," said Charles with dignity, "but not when I think what's suggested is destroying the sense of the whole play.''

The black eyes sizzled up at him. "It is not impossible for this production to be recast," the director hissed.

"Oh, yes, it is," said a cool, unemotional voice. Thank God, thought Charles, that the Asphodel accountant was once again monitoring rehearsals. "Budget doesn't allow it. Sorry, Alex, you work with the cast you've been given. They're all contracted, so, except in case of illness or accident, they all do the full four months—okay?''

Charles Paris met the stare of Alexandru's ferocious black eyes and could see the rich variety of illnesses and accidents they were wishing on him.

EIGHT

CHARLES WAS ANNOYED. For many reasons. Not least among them was that Alexandru Radulescu was efficient. All the arguments Charles wanted to bring forward—that this endless mastication of the text and addition of gratuitous business slowed down the whole production process—were defused by the fact that the schedule was well up to time. Considering his late start on the production, and the amount of new stuff he was bringing into it, Alexandru Radulescu was showing himself to be a very well-organized director.

Even, Charles Paris was grudgingly forced to admit, a rather good director. Not for this show of course, not for *Twelfth Night.* Nor in fact for any show where the text was important. But for the presentation of spectacle, of individual theatrical moments independent of a play's overall structure or the internal logic of characters, Radulescu came up with the goods. This guy should be directing musicals, thought Charles sourly. It wouldn't matter there.

But still his major source of annoyance was the way the director imposed interpretation on the text. In the second week of rehearsal, Alexandru became obsessed with the sexual ambiguity of Viola and Sebastian.

"They express, you see, the male/female duality that is inherent in all of us. They look identical, and yet one is male and the other female. Yet, at the same time, both are attracted to their own sex. And both can inspire attraction in their own sex. I feel this is something we need to explore.''

Charles had become very wary of the director's use of the word *explore*. It invariably led to the discovery of something that had never been there in the first place. But there was no dissent from either of the two characters who were being discussed, or from anyone watching the rehearsal. The three who seemed always to be on hand, Tottie Roundwood, Benzo Ritter, and Talya Northcott, nodded enthusiastically at Alexandru's latest suggestion. Presumably they all paid such rapt attention because they hoped to pick up from the Romanian's table crumbs of genius that might help their theatrical development. Such an idea seemed to Charles excusable in the naive youngsters; Tottie he would have thought was old enough to know better.

''Now,'' the director announced, ''I think it will help enormously if Viola and Sebastian play some of each other's scenes.''

''What!'' Sally Luther was quick to pounce on this idea. Was Alexandru suggesting that they share up the scenes between them? She had come a long way on the path of her rebuilt career to get the part of Viola. A leading part. She wasn't about to sacrifice any of the character's preciously won lines. Sebastian was an important, but minor, character in the play—even when he was being played by the star of ITV's *Air-Sea Rescue*.

The star in question, Russ Lavery, was, unsurprisingly, much more intrigued by the suggestion. "I think it could be good, Alex. Exploring the duality of the other character could give us a new dimension on how we play our own parts."

"Yes, that is my idea."

"I can't see why you're not keen, Sally," said Russ ingenuously.

She ignored him, but demanded suspiciously, "Alex, what are we talking about here—testing this out as a kind of rehearsal method or actually playing some of each other's scenes in performance?"

"Oh, only as a rehearsal method," the director reassured her. But the pensive expression on his face added an unspoken gloss: "For the time being."

And, to Charles's annoyance, the idea did work rather well. Russ Lavery sat in on rehearsals for Viola's scenes and every now and then took over for a run. Sally Luther did the same on Sebastian's scenes. It was a gimmick, but it enriched both performances. Their speech patterns and body language grew more alike. The concept that in Illyria the twins could be mistaken for each other became less fanciful.

And, again to Charles's annoyance, the experiment was somehow fitted in without putting the rest of the production behind schedule. Much as he would have liked to dismiss Alexandru Radulescu as a time-wasting poseur, he couldn't.

IT WAS an afternoon rehearsal in the third week. Outside the rain fell, matching Charles's mood. The first week's atmosphere of excitement had dissipated. Perhaps it would have gone anyway by this stage of the production, but Charles couldn't help feeling wistful for the days when Gavin Scholes had been in charge.

What upset him was being out on a limb. While he had never been one of those actors who can see nothing outside the show he's currently working on, Charles Paris had always been a popular member of the companies he was in. Not one of the most boisterous ones, a bit quiet sometimes—possibly even a loner—but one of the team. What Alexandru Radulescu had achieved was to make him unpopular.

The trouble was that the rest of the cast had been charmed by the director, colonized, subsumed. They had begun to share Alexandru Radulescu's own self-belief. They thought his ideas were good. They thought *Twelfth Night* would be a better production for its director-transplant.

Even Sally Luther, once she had been assured none of her lines were at risk, had started to get excited about the changes.

Only Charles Paris and John B. Murgatroyd held out for the old ways, and John B.'s allegiance was definitely wavering. Charles knew the attitude he'd taken wasn't doing his image in the company any good. It showed his age, his inflexibility. He would overhear cast members talking about how exciting it was to "get a different perspective on a classic, rather than just rely on old-fashioned storytelling." Then he would look away to avoid their gaze of mild contempt at someone who still valued "old-fashioned storytelling."

He also knew that ultimately his intransigence wasn't helping his cause. Although Alexandru Radulescu's directorial method relied on a cataclysmic clash of styles, the one style that would stick out like a sore thumb amidst all the innovation would be the traditional. And Charles was giving a deliberately traditional performance.

He couldn't see quite how the problem would resolve itself. Come the performance, Charles Paris would look as if he were in an entirely different play from the rest of the cast. The fact that he still felt confident he'd be in *Twelfth Night,* while the rest were in something else entirely, would not lessen the incongruity.

For many of the younger members of the cast, this was their first Shakespeare, anyway. Actors such as Benzo Ritter and Talya Northcott felt no obligation to preserve anything because they weren't aware that anything needed preserving. So long as Alexandru Radulescu gave each a few individual moments of flashy theatricality, then everything was fine by them.

So what should Charles do—knuckle under, sacrifice his pride, give a performance as Sir Toby Belch that he knew to be totally wrong, and support Alexandru Radulescu's conspiracy to upstage Shakespeare?

Something of that order might have to happen eventually, but Charles Paris was determined to resist the moment as long as possible.

He was also feeling low about Frances. There had been no more direct confrontations, she had been polite—even pleasant—to him, but he got the feeling she was counting the days till he'd be off to Great Wensham and out of her hair.

Perhaps he was being paranoid about that. What was undeniably true was that she hadn't yet readmitted him to her bed.

OFF THE MAIN HALL where they rehearsed, there was a little scullery that the company called the "green room." The name was appropriate. There was the same atmosphere as backstage, the same coffee jars and cups and spoons, the same sugar spills and biscuit tins.

Usually there was also the same assemblage of actors and actresses, sprawled over chairs sipping coffee, perched against tables bitching about their agents, hunched over crosswords, books, or knitting. But Charles Paris was alone when he went in there that afternoon.

Everyone else was watching the rehearsal. They wanted to see Alexandru Radulescu's latest experiment. It was act 3, scene 3, the first entrance of Sebastian and Antonio, and Alex (as they all now sycophantically called him) had decided he wanted Sally Luther to play Sebastian, "just for this run, you understand, love, just for this run."

Sally, since the exercise involved her having more lines rather than less, readily agreed. And Russ Lavery, after looking momentarily miffed, also fell in with the suggestion. He was, after all, a serious actor "getting back to his roots in the theatre." Directorial experiment excited him; when next interviewed for *TV*

Times, he'd tell them how much he enjoyed "playing with ideas in the rehearsal room, just picking something up and seeing how far you can run with it."

The cast, fascinated to see how Alex's latest invention would work, clustered around to watch the two-handed scene. Even John B. Murgatroyd stayed, wistfully—now almost desperately—wanting to hunt with the pack. Only Charles Paris emphasized his isolation by making for the green room. He'd hoped to slip out unnoticed, but everyone saw him go.

The kettle was empty. He filled and switched it on. Waiting for it to boil, he flicked moodily through the pile of books that someone, trying to tidy the place up, had piled on a central table.

Most of it was predictable rehearsal reading. A Dick Francis. A Joanna Trollope. A compendium of crosswords. A dog-eared analysis of Nostradamus's predictions. Some swot had even brought in *Shakespeare's Festive Comedy* to do some background reading on *Twelfth Night.*

But the book that didn't fit, and the one that interested Charles, was old and green-covered, probably a late-nineteenth-century publication.

It was *An Elementary Handbook of British Fungi* by William Delisle Hay, F.R.G.S.

And there was a torn-paper marker in the chapter entitled "On the Chemistry and Toxicology of Fungi."

NINE

THERE WAS A BREAK in rehearsal and all the company came milling in. They made coffee and formed little knots of chatter round the green room. Vasile Bogdan and Tottie Roundwood expatiated enthusiastically on Alexandru Radulescu's latest ideas. Sally Luther and Benzo Ritter were huddled in deep but inaudible conversation on a sofa in the far corner. Other actors loudly acted and emoted. Charles watched closely over the rim of his coffee cup, but nobody claimed the book on British fungi.

The rehearsal recommenced, but he stayed behind to maintain his vigil, until summoned by a rather testy assistant stage manager. Sir Toby Belch was late for his entrance with Maria and Fabian in act 3, scene 4. Malvolio had been left suspended at the end of his monologue and the momentum of the action had been lost. Everyone was waiting for him.

As Charles scurried shamefacedly into position, he could feel the general disapproval. And, it may have been paranoia, but he could have sworn he heard someone muttering "not so good after lunch these days." Which was annoying because he hadn't actually had a drink that lunchtime.

As a result he was flustered and cocked up his opening line. Instead of "Which way is he, in the name of sanctity?'' his mouth said, ''Which name is he, in the way of sanctity?''

''God, that doesn't even make sense,'' Alexandru Radulescu said contemptuously. ''What can a director do when he's saddled with actors who don't even understand the text?''

This was an infuriating criticism for Charles, given his love of Shakespeare. But it was also, in the current circumstances, unanswerable. Alexandru had scored a point and enlisted yet more company support against Charles Paris.

They played the scene, and Charles knew he wasn't doing it well. Not nearly as well as he'd played it in previous rehearsals. The trouble was that the general resistance to his performance was getting to him. Charles shared the undermining weakness of far too many people—he liked to be liked. An atmosphere of disapprobation wormed away at his confidence. He started to wonder whether perhaps he should be playing Sir Toby as Alexandru demanded. He even started to wonder whether he actually had any talent at all as an actor.

Act 3, scene 4, is a long one, and one of Sir Toby Belch's biggest, as he hurries on-and offstage setting up the elaborate mechanics of the duel between Sir Andrew Aguecheek and Cesario. Charles usually enjoyed playing the scene, but not that afternoon. His mind was in the green room, wondering who, if anyone, had picked up his or her book on British fungi.

When, at last, he could leave the stage, his exit line

proved prophetic: "I dare lay any money, 'twill be nothing yet."

For nothing was what he found. The book of British fungi was no longer in the green room. And there was no way of knowing who had reclaimed it.

Charles Paris could not remove from his mind the image of the dining room at Chailey Ferrars, of Gavin Scholes swallowing down a mushroom tartlet.

DOING THE full run of the play meant inevitably that they overran their designated rehearsal time, but this gave rise to no objections. Alexandru Radulescu, showing surprising awareness of British union rules, kept checking with the company's Equity representative that he had permission to continue. The Romanian showed an annoying degree of tact for someone Charles would like to have dismissed as an insensitive megalomaniac.

The run wound through to its end, gathering momentum. Sir Toby Belch did the little he had to do in act 5. He approached, "bleeding, led by the Clown," and let out his few petulantly drunken lines before being taken off to have his wound dressed. Again, Charles felt unhappy about what he was doing. And again he was getting paranoid. He felt sure, after Sir Toby had said, "I hate a drunken rogue," he heard a voice murmur, "Takes one to know one."

The play's final loose ends were tied up in neat matrimonial bows—though of course, this being an Alexandru Radulescu production, the bows were not tied very tight. The impression was left that after the play's end the characters faced lives of serial infidelity—with partners of both sexes.

Then Chad Pearson, alone onstage, came forward to sing "When that I was and a little tiny boy…" The words, to Charles's continuing annoyance, remained indistinct, but the moment was still theatrical, its wailing Indian music compounding the melancholy that lies at the heart of *Twelfth Night.*

The general view at the end of the run was that it had gone well for this stage of the production. There was even a beginning of communal excitement, restoring the feeling of the first week under Gavin Scholes. Since it was late, a popular suggestion spread of everyone going off to "an Indian for a bite to eat."

There was much discussion as to how many were going. A hard core committed themselves immediately, while some thought they ought to get back home, but lingered and were persuaded. Sally Luther was among these.

"I really shouldn't," she said. "My flat's in a hell of a mess and we're going to be away for months."

"Oh, go on, do come," urged Benzo Ritter. He sounded truculent, his tone implying that she'd be letting him down if she refused.

Sally looked across at the boy and grimaced. "Oh, all right, I'll come."

Benzo looked marginally more cheerful.

Charles was torn. He didn't really want to go. He'd enjoyed many riotous postperformance dinners over the years, but he wasn't in the mood that evening. Also he had a vague recollection of having hinted to

Frances that he might take her out for a meal. He was always better on a one-to-one basis, and a little fence-mending with his wife was certainly overdue.

Also, he wasn't that keen on Indian food. That is to say, he liked it while he was eating it, but he didn't like the aftertaste that seemed to stay in his mouth for the ensuing twenty-four hours. And, pathetically, his stomach was very old-fashioned about spicy food. As a result, he would never go to an Indian restaurant by choice and, on the rare occasions when he did, always had to be guided through the unfamiliar menu.

So there were a lot of arguments for just slipping away at the end of rehearsals with a casual, "Got to meet someone for dinner. See you in the morning."

Against that was, once more, the dreadful pressure of wanting to be liked. Fences certainly needed to be mended with Frances, but he didn't want to break any more with the *Twelfth Night* company. These were the people he was going to be spending the next four months with. Some kind of working relationship with them had to be recaptured. Charles Paris didn't relish being ostracized; it wasn't his style.

A measure of how far his isolation had already gone was that, as all the cast shuffled off chattering and pulling on their coats, it was only John B. Murgatroyd who asked, "You're not going to come, are you, Charles?"

If ever there was a question expecting the answer no, that was it.

"Yes," Charles Paris replied. "I'll come."

"So LET ME get this right—is it the *khurma* that's mild and the *vindaloo* hot?"

"Yes, yes, yes," said John B. Murgatroyd dismissively, and turned to his right to talk to Talya Northcott.

"And the *madras* is somewhere in the middle?" asked Charles. He felt rather pathetic for not knowing. And he also worried that John B. Murgatroyd was sitting next to him only out of pity. His friend'd much rather be the other side of the table, in the raucous sycophantic crowd that surrounded Alexandru Radulescu. The director was flanked by Russ Lavery and Vasile Bogdan. Sally Luther and Tottie Roundwood spread out from them. Benzo Ritter was beside Tottie; he looked a little marginalized—rather the way Charles felt.

Chad Pearson, seated beside Sally, was in the middle of some scatological anecdote about a slow-witted Jamaican immigrant. It was all right for him. He was black. Anything he said against black people was politically acceptable.

Chad reached his punch line with immaculate timing, and the area around him erupted with laughter. When it subsided, Alexandru Radulescu was full of congratulations. "Excellent, Chad, excellent. You are very good comedy actor. It is a pity that Feste doesn't have more comedy in the play. Maybe we work out some extra business to use your talents properly, eh?"

Chad Pearson responded to this with some line in his dumb-Jamaican patois, which again set the table on a roar. Charles wasn't near enough to hear what was said. He hadn't been near enough to hear more than the odd word of the original story. His spirits sank lower. Pity Osbert Sitwell had used the title *Laughter in the Next Room* for a volume of autobiography. It would have suited Charles Paris's memoirs. Not of course that there was anything worth remembering in his life. A long timetable of missed buses and wrong roads followed.

Oh, God, he must get out of this cycle of self-recrimination. There was an unhealthy indulgence in it, a picking away at the scabs of his discontent, willing them to reinfect themselves.

A waiter was slowly working his way round the table, taking orders. There was so much hilarity, so much backchat, so much flamboyance, so many changes of mind, that it was hard for him to pin the diners down to final decisions, particularly on the minutiae of *bhajees, nans, chapatis,* and *pappadums.*

"I must just nip off to the gents," John B. Murgatroyd announced. "Order me a chicken *vindaloo,* Charles. With a *tarka dall.* And *pillau* rice. And, as for you, my dear"—he turned a sexy beam on Talya Northcott—"I'm sure Charles will keep you conversationally on the boil till my return."

The pretty little actress gave Charles a token grin and then turned determinedly to talk to the person on her right.

I'm too old, he thought. Why should I imagine a young woman would be interested in me? Why should I imagine any woman would be interested in me?

Even Frances. He'd really screwed up with Frances.

The one lifeline that was offered for his declining years and he had deliberately swum away from it. He should be with her at that moment, making it up with her, telling her how much she meant to him, telling her that she was the only woman he'd ever really loved and that he'd definitely try in the future to—

"Yes, please, sir?" The waiter's voice broke into this self-indulgent spiral of misery. "Have you decided?"

"Oh, yes." John B.'s instructions had completely vanished from Charles's head. He grasped at the menu, hoping it would remind him. "Now my friend wants a *tarka* something. Not *tarka* the otter, I know, but—"

"*Tarka dall,*" supplied the waiter, and wrote it down.

"And he wanted a...*vindaloo,* I think."

"Prawn *vindaloo* is very good, sir."

"Yes, fine. And I'll have the...which is the mild one?"

"*Khurma* is mild. Or"—a note of contempt came into the waiter's voice—"*dupiaza* is so mild it hardly deserves the name of a curry."

"Chicken *dupiaza* for me, please," said Charles wimpishly. He also wanted to order some of those nice crispy round things, but he couldn't remember whether they were *chapati* or *pappadum.* Unwilling to show himself up further, he didn't ask for either.

"And boiled rice for both of you, yes?"

"Er, yes, fine," said Charles, and took another long swallow of wine.

He knew there was little chance of shifting his mood, but at least he could numb it with alcohol. Pity he hadn't had the chance to put down a few large Bell's before they got to the restaurant. Wine worked, but it took so much longer. And you needed a lot more of it. Charles Paris refilled his glass.

THE LARGE ORDER from the *Twelfth Night* company seemed to have thrown the restaurant into confusion. Maybe they were short-staffed, maybe there was some crisis in the kitchen... For whatever reason, the food took a long time to arrive. The actors drank more, ordered extra bottles, and grew ever rowdier.

As a result, there was a lot more confusion—genuine and engineered—when the food finally came. People couldn't remember what they'd ordered. Some mischievously claimed things they hadn't ordered, while others rejected dishes that they had ordered. It was the kind of mayhem that Indian restaurateurs are presumably used to when they have in a large party of overexcited thespians.

"Who's the chicken *madras?*... King prawn *biryani* anyone?... Whose are the *dupiazas?*... Someone's stolen my *nan.*... Oy, get the chutney down here.... I'm missing a *chapati.*... I definitely did order a *sag aloo.*" The sound level rose higher and higher.

But slowly order was imposed on the orders. The joke of pretending to have got the wrong food wore thin, metal dishes were reallocated around the table, wineglasses recharged, and the serious business of eating began.

"What the hell's this?" John B. Murgatroyd demanded when the only meal left that could possibly be his appeared in front of him. "Charles, what did you order me?"

"*Vindaloo*—that's what you wanted, isn't it?"

"Yes, chicken *vindaloo,* not prawn. For God's sake, I'm allergic to shellfish. If I eat these now, I'll be throwing up all over the place in three hours' time."

"Oh, I am sorry. I wasn't concentrating. Look, you have mine. Mine's chicken."

John B. Murgatroyd scrutinized the proffered dish dubiously. "What is that?"

"Chicken *dupi*...duppy-doopy-something?"

"*Dupiaza?*" John B. had caught the waiter's note of contempt.

"Yes."

"Oh, God." Charles's order was picked up and waved over the table as John B. Murgatroyd shouted out, "Anybody fancy swapping a chicken *dupiaza* for something stronger?"

Howls of derision—"I've already got one," "No way," "Forget it"—greeted this suggestion.

"Order something else," said Charles. "I'll pay. Look, I'm sorry if—"

"God, no. If it takes them this long to get things cooked, I'll be waiting all night. I'll eat this."

John B. Murgatroyd dumped a portion of chicken *dupiaza* onto his plate, then saw the rice. "Oh, shit. I did say order *pillau.*"

"I'm sorry. I—"

But John B. Murgatroyd turned his back on his

friend and spent the rest of the meal strenuously and unambiguously chatting up Talya Northcott.

Leaving Charles feeling even more wretched. Particularly as he found the prawn *vindaloo* inedibly hot.

JOHN B. MURGATROYD clearly thought he was on to a winner. The intentions of his chatting up became more overt as the evening progressed. He spoke to Charles only once, when Talya had slipped away to make a phone call.

"I think the old John B. magic's working again," he said leeringly. "I think a serious, steamy bonking session is going to prove unavoidable. God, it's hell, you know, being fatally attractive to women"—he grinned smugly—"but I've learned to live with it. Ah, my dear," he greeted the returning Handmaiden, "you just put your beautiful little bottom back down there."

Why is it, Charles asked himself bitterly, that one always feels jealous of someone who's clearly about to score? It doesn't make any difference if you find the object of their attentions utterly repulsive. It doesn't even matter how well your own sex life's going at that precise moment...not of course that mine's going at all right now. His mind readily, even eagerly, supplied the gloomy thoughts, and the cycle of self-hatred started up again.

They'd got to the stage of bill-paying. By now everyone was keen to leave. Those who didn't reckon they were on a promise like John B. Murgatroyd were simply tired. It'd been a long day's rehearsal, and they had to start again at ten in the morning. Another ten

days and *Twelfth Night* would be opening at Chailey
Ferrars. They all needed to conserve their energy.

Dividing up the bill was, as ever, complicated, and
the communal mood was by now scratchier. The company's two teetotalers objected to contributing to the
wine; the vegetarians, Tottie Roundwood and Talya
Northcott, insisted they'd only ordered small vegetable
curries; all the usual wrangles developed. And, as always, somebody—in this case the company manager—produced a calculator and started working it all
out.

Sally Luther, exasperated, slammed a twenty-pound
note down on the table and left. Benzo Ritter's eyes
followed her like a rejected spaniel's. She hadn't even
said good-bye to him. Charles felt a moment of sympathy for the young actor. Infatuation's tough when
you're that age, he recollected.

"I'll pay for yours," said John B. Murgatroyd,
flamboyantly placing a twenty- and a ten-pound note
on Talya's side-plate.

"Oh, thank you very much," she giggled.

John B.'s proprietorial hand was on her shoulder.
"Come on, let's move. See you, Charles," he threw
back as they strolled to the door.

Wistfully, Charles watched them across the room.
Then Olivia's Handmaiden walked up to an elegantly
dressed woman in her sixties, who was standing by
the coatrack. Introductions were made and the new
arrival graciously shook John B. Murgatroyd's hand.
Talya Northcott also shook her host politely by the

hand; then she and the woman who was undoubtedly "Mummy" left.

Charles Paris did not need the explanation John B. gave as he came stomping back to the table; Charles had read it all in the little pantomime by the door. "Only rung up her bloody, sodding mother, hadn't she? Oh, shit! Fucking, pissing shit!"

"All-round entertainer," said Charles.

"What?"

"Well, shit that can fuck and piss could surely get bookings at any venue in the..." But John B.'s face suggested he was in no mood to pursue verbal fantasies. Charles looked at his watch. "Pubs're still open. Fancy a quick one?"

"That's what I thought Talya bloody Northcott was going to say," John B. Murgatroyd muttered. "Oh, yes, what the hell? Let's see how many quick ones we can fit in before they close."

TEN

"WHAT WE'RE DOING isn't working, you know," said John B. Murgatroyd as he sat down with their second round of drinks. The pub had recently been refurbished, decked out with all those brass rails, colored-glass lamps, and sporting prints that are meant to give character, but are now so familiar they drain it all away.

"It *is*," Charles protested. He took a substantial swallow from his large Bell's. "We are doing the play as Shakespeare intended it to be done. We are making *sense* of our scenes."

"We're still sticking out like sore thumbs in this production."

"That's the production's fault, not ours. Everything else is just flashy theatrical tricks; we are actually telling the story."

"Still sticking out like sore thumbs." John B. Murgatroyd took a reflective swig from his second pint.

"So what are you suggesting—that we cave in, do as Alexandru tells us, make nonsense of the play?"

"Well—"

"Listen, I'm not denying he's talented. He is. He has some very good ideas. *Some* very good ideas. But not all his ideas are good. And it needs someone to stand up to him and tell him that. He'll listen."

"I doubt it."

"He listens to that guy from Asphodel. When he was told he couldn't change the sets and costumes, okay, Alexandru stamped his little foot, but he accepted it. Thank God he did. Otherwise no doubt we'd be doing *Twelfth Night* in cycling shorts and kimonos. But, you see, a firm hand works. We've got to stand up to him about the way we play our characters."

"We just look wrong. I was noticing during the run this afternoon. The two of us looked totally out of place."

"That's because the place is wrong, not our performances."

"Maybe. It doesn't matter which, anyway. It's still going to give the audience a strange feeling, as if they're watching something unfinished."

"Listen, John B." The alcohol had made Charles more forceful and confessional than he might have been under other circumstances. "My career as an actor hasn't been great. I've had my chances, okay. Most of them I've screwed up. I've never made it to the top rank. At my age it's very unlikely now that I ever will. I can accept that. I *have* accepted that.

"But it doesn't mean I've run out of ambition. There are still things I want to do professionally, still things I believe I *can* do professionally. And playing Sir Toby Belch is one of them. It's a part I've always wanted, and one I know I can play well. Under Gavin I was getting the chance to play it well. Now that's being threatened. It's impossible for me to give a good performance with Alexandru directing."

John B. Murgatroyd shook his head ruefully. "The production was looking pretty good this afternoon. Even you must admit that."

"Yes, moments looked okay, I agree. Some of the effects are stunning, but it's all at the expense of the play—and at the expense of the actors. You know, no one in the cast is going to get any decent notices out of this."

"Well, I don't know. I'd have thought—"

"All the notices will be about the production. They'll talk about 'Alexandru Radulescu's radical new interpretation,' 'Radulescu's brave vision.' Directing for him's nothing more or less than an ego trip."

John B. Murgatroyd squirmed uncomfortably. "But if it *works*..."

"Do I gather from this, John B., that you're about to start playing Sir Andrew Aguecheek differently?"

"Well...maybe."

So Charles Paris had lost his one supporter in the *Twelfth Night* company. From now on it was just he against the massed forces of Alexandru Radulescu's creatures.

There was a morose silence while they sipped their drinks.

Charles finally reopened the conversation. "Going back to what I was saying about Gavin's illness..."

His friend groaned. "Oh, no, Charles! All I want to do for the rest of this evening is to get smashed out of my skull. I don't think I've got the energy for any more conspiracy theorizing."

"No, listen..." And Charles told John B. Murgatroyd about the book he'd found in the green room.

"Well, so what? So...somebody in the company's interested in British fungi...or possibly in old books, who can say? I don't think we should drag in the CID quite yet, Charles."

"But, taken in conjunction with what I heard Vasile say to Alexandru, *and* the fact that I saw Gavin eating a mushroom tartlet the day before he was taken ill..."

"Pure coincidence."

"I'm not so sure. I think I'm going to go and have a word with Gavin."

"Fine. Good. You do that. Give him my love." Across the room the landlord, with a lack of charisma that matched his pub's decor, rang a bell and dolefully called, "Time." John B. watched him with disappointment. "Why do they always do that just when you're getting a taste for the stuff?"

"Mm, rotten," Charles agreed. Then an idea came to him. "Tell you what...you could come back to my place for a nightcap."

"Your place? But you're miles down Westbourne Grove way, aren't you?"

"Not at the moment. I'm staying in my wife's flat."

"Ah." John B. Murgatroyd was attracted by the idea. "Are you sure she won't mind?"

"Oh, no. She won't mind."

FRANCES WAS far too well brought up to let John B. Murgatroyd see if she did mind, but Charles knew her well enough to detect a slight resentment on their arrival. It wasn't so much the fact of his appearing on her doorstep at half-past eleven, clearly drunk, in the company of someone she'd never met before, also clearly drunk; Charles got the feeling it might have more to do with his not having been there earlier to take her out for dinner. Maybe what he'd thought of as a to-be-confirmed possibility had been a definite arrangement. That would certainly justify Frances's frostiness.

But he admired the way she didn't let on to John B. His friend was made to feel extremely welcome and not allowed to sense any edge in her refusal to join them for another drink on the grounds that she had to be at school early in the morning.

Charles somewhat mournfully watched her go. He had a feeling that, when he did finally make it to bed, he'd find her bedroom door once again closed. All in all, he had made rather a cock-up of the evening.

''Lovely woman,'' John B. Murgatroyd commented as he slumped onto her sofa. ''You never told me you were married. Recent thing, is it?''

''No, we've been married quite a time,'' replied Charles, unsnapping the top of a new bottle of Bell's. ''You all right on the Scotch?''

''You bet. Seal in the beer. So how long?''

''How long?''

''How long've you been married?''

''Oh, God.'' Charles toted it up in his head. Surely it couldn't be that long. He rechecked the figures. No, it was. He told John B.

''Jesuuuus! Lots of people don't live that long.''

"No. Well…"

"And you've actually been together all that time?"

"Mm. Pretty much." Charles handed across a large Scotch. "I mean, inevitably there have been gaps…with me working in the theatre and…you know…"

"Well, good on you, mate. And good on her too, eh?" John B. Murgatroyd raised his glass in salutation. He was already too fuddled to ask why, if Charles was locked into an ongoing marriage to Frances, he actually lived on his own in a bed-sitter in Hereford Road.

THEY DRANK ON steadily, their conversation, in the way of such conversations, circling round the same points and recycling them. They both agreed, many times, that *Twelfth Night* was a "bloody good play." They both bemoaned, many times, that they hadn't been allowed to act their parts as they ought to be acted. John B., who had by now given up all pretense that he was going to continue his resistance to Alexandru Radulescu's ideas, said dolefully, many times, how little he was going to enjoy the rest of the rehearsal period. While Charles Paris asserted vehemently, and many times, that he was going to continue playing Sir Toby Belch the way Shakespeare had written the character.

It was about half-past one. They were at that stage when the conversation filled with lacunae as one or other dozed off. Getting a taxi for John B. had been mentioned at least four times, but the effort of moving to the phone seemed insuperable to both of them.

Then, suddenly, John B. Murgatroyd sat bolt upright on the sofa. His hand shot up to cover his mouth. "My God, I think I'm going to be sick!"

Charles stumbled to his feet. "I'll show you where the bathroom is."

But John B. didn't make it that far. In the middle of Frances's neat hall, all over her new oatmeal carpet, he began to spew his guts out. He clutched at his stomach and sank down against the wall, but still the flow spurted from his mouth.

Charles heard the door of Frances's bedroom open behind him and turned apologetically. She was standing, belting up her dressing gown, with a hard look in her eyes.

"I'm sorry. Just a little bit too much to drink. He's not usually...," Charles babbled.

Frances moved across to assess the damage to her carpet. Charles followed uselessly behind her.

"Good God!"

The shock in Frances's voice made him look down. Amidst the mess that still pumped relentlessly out of John B. Murgatroyd's mouth, Charles could see bright flecks of blood.

"I'm going to call an ambulance," Frances announced.

ELEVEN

"THEY WANT TO keep me in for tests," said John B. Murgatroyd sullenly.

He looked drained, wrung out like an old floorcloth. Presumably the drip that fed into his arm was part of the hospital rehydration process.

It was the evening of the following day, the first time the patient had been deemed well enough to have visitors. Anyway, Charles couldn't have got to the hospital earlier. He'd been locked into a heavy day of hungover rehearsal. Without John B. there for support, his own performance had seemed even more at odds with what was going on around him.

For that day an assistant stage manager had read in Sir Andrew Aguecheek's lines, but with just over a week till the show opened, a decision about the future had to be made quickly. Alexandru Radulescu had agreed to hold fire on this until the following morning. John B. Murgatroyd's consultant was going to see him then and would pronounce on the actor's chances of getting back into the show. Looking at the shriveled figure sunken into pillows, Charles Paris didn't put those chances very high.

"Have they given any suggestion of what they think it might be?"

John B. Murgatroyd shrugged feebly. "'Food poisoning' 's as far as they'll go at the moment. They've sent off some of my stomach contents to the labs for...biopsy, is that the word?''

"I'm surprised they could find any contents left in there."

John B. didn't even smile. He was very low.

"Still, if it was food poisoning, probably as well you chucked it all out." There was a silence. "And you've no idea what it might have been?"

"You were there, Charles. Your guess is as good as mine. Something in the curry, I suppose. If I'd had the prawns, I wouldn't have been surprised—I've always been allergic to them. Still, chicken can be dodgy if it's been reheated, can't it? Or maybe I've developed an exciting new allergy to something I've never been allergic to before. I don't know." He spoke without interest.

"And the thought hasn't occurred to you that it might be something else?"

"Well, the ward sister puts it down purely and simply to alcohol. I thought I'd flushed most of that out of my system, but apparently I was still reeking of the stuff when I was brought in here. A somewhat puritanical lady, the ward sister—as I'm discovering."

"We had a lot last night, but not more than we've had on plenty of other occasions without worse effects than a sore head."

"Exactly." John B. Murgatroyd nuzzled sideways into his pillow and yawned weakly. It was a fairly unambiguous hint that Charles should leave.

"But you don't think there's anything suspicious about it?"

"What, Charles?" A light of understanding came into the sick man's eye. "Oh, for God's sake," he said wearily. "You're not still on about that. Leave it alone."

"But it's getting more than a coincidence. Gavin Scholes, whose departure opens up the possibility of Alexandru Radulescu taking over, suddenly gets ill with abdominal pains. You, who're one of the two actors who's opposing the way Alexandru's directing the show, suddenly get ill with abdominal pains. Call me a conspiracy theorist if you like, but at least there seem to be grounds for my having a conspiracy theory."

"Charles, as I said, leave it alone. It's happened. I'm ill. Whatever the reason, it looks like I'm out of the show."

Charles began a token remonstrance, assurance that his friend would soon be fine and—

"Don't bother. Look at me. There's no way I'm going to open in *Twelfth Night* next week, is there?"

"Well…"

"So I've got to come to terms with that. It's a real bugger—I was looking forward to doing the show—but there it is."

"Oh, come on. Surely you want to get even with whoever did this to you."

"I don't think anyone did anything to me. It was just bad luck."

"At the very least, you could sue the restaurant or get the health inspectors out to them or—"

"Charles, I don't want to do anything. I want to forget about it, and just get better—okay?"

Charles Paris looked at his friend's exhausted face. The freckles stood out unnaturally against the surrounding pallor. It was no longer a sparkling, comical face. John B. Murgatroyd looked crumpled and defeated. And, Charles suddenly realized, another emotion also was on display.

"You're frightened, John B., aren't you?"

The anemic attempt to shrug off this suggestion was more telling than an admission.

"But if you're frightened, that must mean you believe there's some truth in what I've been saying. You wouldn't be frightened unless—"

"Charles, I'm frightened because I'm forty-four years old and for the first time in my life I've come up against the possibility of real illness. Suddenly losing control of your body like that is a real shock. Abdominal bleeding could be a symptom of any number of extremely nasty conditions—one at least of which begins with the letter *C*. If I look frightened, I'd say I have every justification for looking frightened."

It was a good speech, but it didn't fool Charles. "No, you're frightened because you think someone in the company poisoned you. That's why you want to lie low, why you don't want to argue. You're afraid if you make a fuss, they'll try again."

"Crap, Charles. And please stop going on about it.

I'm feeling really shitty. All I want to do is close my eyes and shut out the world.''

"Yes, yes, okay.'' Charles began to feel guilty for hounding a man in such reduced health. "I'm sorry. I'll be off. See if I can make my peace with Frances.''

"Oh. Look, I'm sorry about her carpet. It came on so suddenly, I just didn't have time to—''

"It's not her carpet I need to make peace with Frances about.''

"Ah. Okay. Right. Well, good luck.''

"Thanks.'' Charles stood up. "Hope you sleep well and...you know, wake feeling better.''

"Yes. Sure I will,'' said John B. Murgatroyd without conviction. "And thanks for coming, mate.''

"No problem.'' Charles moved awkwardly toward the door.

"Of course, there is one thing...'' John B. Murgatroyd's weak voice stopped Charles.

"Hm?''

"If one did go along with your crap conspiracy theory...''

"Yes?''

"...and really believed that someone in the *Twelfth Night* company put poison on some of the food last night...''

Charles was silent, alert.

"...and deliberately targeted the chicken *dupiaza*...well, I didn't order that. So it wasn't me they were out to get, was it? They were out to get you.''

CHARLES WAS determined not to have a drink until Frances came back. She was late. It was agony.

But he needed to talk to her. And he needed to be sober when he talked to her. In less than a week he'd be off to Great Wensham; then all over the place for three months. Things had to be sorted out before then.

He was sitting in the middle of the sofa, feeling very conspicuous and only partially dressed without a drink in his hand, when he heard the front door. It was half-past twelve. Frances came into the sitting room, as if to turn off the lights. He noticed she was smartly dressed, in softer and more feminine style than her headmistress mode. She reacted with surprise to his presence and asked tartly, "Couldn't sleep?"

"No, I just...I wanted to talk."

"Oh. Really?" Her eyes immediately moved to her watch. "Can't be long. I'm exhausted and the school will open the same time in the morning regardless."

"Yes." He had to get the important fact in quickly. "I haven't had a drink all day."

"Well, there's a novelty. Let's hope Arthur Bell and Sons can survive this temporary blip in their profits."

She still didn't sit down, but lingered by the door as if keen to be away.

"I've been to see John B."

"How is he?"

"Pretty washed-out."

"But conscious?"

"Oh, yes. On a drip. The consultant's going to see him in the morning. Know his immediate prospects then."

She nodded. "They got any idea what it was?"

"Talk of food poisoning." In the past Charles had

sometimes shared with Frances his suspicions about criminal activities; now there were more important subjects to discuss. "I don't think he's going to make it for the show."

"Ah. Bad luck for him."

"Mm. You have a good evening?"

"Yes, thank you."

She deliberately hadn't volunteered any more information, which should have been a signal to him, but Charles couldn't stop himself from asking, "What did you do?"

"Had dinner with an American friend."

An interrogative "Ah?"

"Someone I met at an international teachers' conference."

"I didn't know teachers had international conferences."

"Well, you learn a little something every day, don't you, Charles? If you ever showed any interest in my work, I might have told you that, as a headmistress, I get invited to an increasing number of conferences of one kind and another."

The rebuke was justified. "And do you go to many of them?"

"If the subject's interesting and I can fit it into my schedule, yes."

"And this American you met tonight...does she teach in the States?"

"He. Yes."

"Ah." A silence loomed between them. "Frances, about what happened last night..."

"I thought we'd just been talking about what happened last night. John B. Murgatroyd's conscious and on a drip."

"I meant before he got ill...the fact that I brought him back here for a drinking session...the fact that I forgot you and I were meant to be going out together...or that it was as definite an arrangement as... It was insensitive."

"Yes," Frances agreed.

"And I wanted to say I'm sorry. And it won't happen again."

"No, I shouldn't think it would."

Charles looked up, blinking with hope. Did she actually believe him? Had she accepted that he really, genuinely intended to turn over a new leaf?

"I shouldn't think it would," Frances went on, "because by this time next week you'll be away doing *Twelfth Night* at wherever it is, and I wouldn't imagine even you would have the gall to do a repeat performance here in one of the intervening evenings."

"Frances—"

"And, after that, who you bring back to drink at wherever you may happen to be staying...won't be my problem."

"Oh, Frances..." He took in the familiar outline of her face and realized how much he loved her. Had always loved her. Would always love her. Tears prickled at his eyes, and he wasn't even drunk. "I really thought we could get back together this time—you know, make it work."

"So did I, Charles," said Frances softly. Then, with

a sharp "Pity we were both wrong," she turned on her heel and left the room.

Charles did have a drink then. Quite a few, actually.

THERE WAS no surprise in the rehearsal room when the message from the hospital came. John B. Murgatroyd was going to be out of action for at least a week, and probably a lot longer. He would be unable to play Sir Andrew Aguecheek for the Great Wensham Festival.

"I have of course been prepared for this eventuality," Alexandru Radulescu announced to the hushed company.

Oh, yes? For how long? Charles wondered.

"And I do not at this stage wish to introduce new members into our cast. We have a good ensemble feeling here. Almost all of us"—Charles looked down to avoid the inevitable glances cast in his direction—"are working together well to make a production that is really going to register with its audience."

If not with lovers of *Twelfth Night,* Charles thought for the thousandth time.

"So I am not going to regard John B.'s accident as a problem. I am going to look on it instead as a positive creative opportunity. It can spur us on to a new pitch of excitement in the show, if we accept the challenge we are offered. So…we will have someone new to play Sir Andrew Aguecheek."

During the pause that Alexandru Radulescu left for dramatic effect, Charles tried to predict who would get promoted. Since he had so many scenes with Sir Andrew, the outcome was of considerable importance for him. Mind you, he didn't think there was much chance of getting anyone who'd play the part right. Even John B. Murgatroyd had been on the verge of defecting to Alexandru Radulescu's camp, and the rest of the company were already firmly installed there.

He looked round the room. Everyone was expectant, but the most feverish glow showed on the faces of the youngest male cast members. Benzo Ritter, in particular, sparkled with anticipation. Charles felt sorry for the boy. He knew how potent the mythology of the theatre is. One day you're a walk-on...one of the leads is taken ill...the director points at you...you rise magnificently to the challenge...and a star is born.

If that was what was going through Benzo Ritter's mind—and it almost certainly was—then he was due for a disappointment. None of the male Attendants or Officers had showed sufficient talent to justify their promotion to a part as important as Sir Andrew Aguecheek. No, the logical thing, Charles reckoned, would be to move Vasile Bogdan up into the role and give Fabian to the best of the walk-ons.

In spite of his arrogance and self-regard, Vasile was a good actor. As Fabian he was in a lot of the Sir Toby/Sir Andrew scenes, so he would be familiar with the lines and moves. He was tall too, which was right for the part. His complexion was a bit dark, but that could be paled down with makeup. And presumably he'd be given John B. Murgatroyd's floppy blond wig, so that his hair could, as the text demands, hang "like flax from a distaff."

Charles didn't relish acting so closely with Vasile. The young man was totally under Alexandru Radulescu's spell; he'd play everything exactly as the director told him. Charles knew he was probably being old-fashioned about it, but he didn't relish the homosexual kiss that would inevitably get grafted on at some point. Also, though he hadn't yet cleared his mind on the subject of poisonings within the company…if there had been any, then Vasile Bogdan was way up any possible list of suspects.

Charles was so carried away in his thoughts that it was a moment before he took in Alexandru Radulescu's next words. "I'd like you to play the part, Chad."

"What!" The word was out of Charles Paris's mouth before he had time to think.

"What's wrong? You have some objection, Charles?" The director's black eyes turned on him, teasing, challenging him to make a fool of himself.

"Well, it's just…"

"I hope you're not suggesting Chad is not good enough to play the part."

"No, not at all. I have a great respect for Chad. He's a very fine actor."

"Thanks, mate." The West Indian beamed a cheery grin at him.

"It's just…"

"What?" asked Alexandru Radulescu, feeding out more line to his victim.

"It's just that Chad's wrong physically."

"Physically?"

"All the references to Sir Andrew in the play are about him being long and thin. Even the name *Aguecheek* suggests he's thin. The first line Sir Toby says about him is 'He's as tall a man as any's in Illyria.' At the end he's described as 'a thin-faced knave.' I mean, Chad, as I say, is a terrific actor...but there's no way you're long and thin, is there?"

He turned his appeal to the subject of the conversation, who grinned again and said, "No way."

"Don't you think you're being a bit literal, Charles?" suggested Alexandru Radulescu gleefully. "Surely what one's trying to do in the theatre is to excite, to surprise the audience by doing something different? They come to the theatre with certain expectations..."

"In this case the expectation that they're going to see *Twelfth Night* by William Shakespeare."

"Okay. And it's up to us to surprise them. They expect Sir Andrew Aguecheek to be tall and thin—then he isn't. They are surprised, yes?"

"Yes, but it's wrong. And it's not just that," Charles plunged on. He knew he was getting into deeper and deeper water, but he couldn't stop himself. His resentment had been building from the moment that Alexandru Radulescu took over the production. "Sir Andrew's meant to be *pale*. That's what *Aguecheek* means. Just before his first entrance, Sir Toby even calls him 'Sir Andrew Agueface,' which is a comment on his washed-out complexion. Then his hair's described as hanging like flax; there's the line about him not having 'so much blood in his liver as

will clog the foot of a flea.' It's obvious that the Sir
Andrew Aguecheek Shakespeare intended was tall,
thin, and anemically pale.''

''Pale?'' echoed Alexandru Radulescu quietly.
''Charles, you're not saying Chad's the wrong color,
are you?''

Which of course *was* what Charles was saying; but
was also, in the theatre's current climate of political
correctness, totally unsayable.

TWELVE

NOW THAT HE was identified not only as an actor unreceptive to the Romanian boy wonder's ideas but also as a racist, Charles Paris's position within the *Twelfth Night* company became even more uncomfortable. Normally, in the week before a show's opening, he would share in the communal mood, the giddy excitements when everything seemed to be coming together, the swooping despairs when it all fell apart. Now, though he was aware of all that was going on around him, Charles felt painfully isolated from the process.

But he still thought he was right. He was still of the opinion that Alexandru Radulescu was systematically destroying the finely tuned comic machinery of *Twelfth Night*. And no amount of pressure toward political correctness would ever convince him that Sir Andrew Aguecheek should be played by a short, tubby West Indian. He had seen some very successful mixed-race casting in Shakespeare productions, but only where the individual actor was right for the individual part. Alexandru Radulescu's choice of Chad Pearson had been simply perverse.

So had his elevation to Chad's part of the Indian sitar player (another disappointment to the dreams of Benzo Ritter). Alexandru's arguments that the most important function of Feste the Clown was to provide music were let down, in Charles's view, by the fact that the Indian could not act for toffee. His accent was so strong that few of his words were comprehensible, particularly in the songs, which were his supposed raison d'être. And his singing style demonstrated none of Chad Pearson's magical charisma.

But Charles was too canny to point any of this out. He'd already offended the Afro-Caribbean contingent; he wasn't about to take on the Asian lobby too.

Even under pressure of the last week of rehearsal, the director still managed to find time to experiment, and Charles was once again forced to grudging admiration for Radulescu's efficiency. Alexandru continued to explore the Viola/Sebastian duality, constantly recasting their scenes in rehearsal so that Sally Luther and Russ Lavery became as familiar with each other's role as they were with their own.

And the benefit of the exercise was evident in both performances. Greater depth and texture came into their interpretations, and the possibility of the one being mistaken for the other became infinitely more plausible.

Yes, even Charles admitted, some of Alexandru Radulescu's ideas were very good indeed. It was the rest of them that drove him mad.

The latest example of the director's sheer gratuitous gimmickry affected the production's wardrobe. Charles had assumed, after the intervention of the Asphodel representative, that at least the sets and costumes were sacrosanct. But he had reckoned without Alexandru Radulescu.

The first hint of trouble came when they were re-hearsing act 2, scene 3, in which the late-night ca-rousing of Sir Toby Belch, Sir Andrew Aguecheek, and the Clown is interrupted by a furious Malvolio entering with the line "My masters, are you mad?"

"This is not working," Alexandru Radulescu inter-rupted, waving his arms discontentedly. "We are not getting enough offense. Why is Malvolio so angry?"

"Because we are making a drunken row late at night in a court that he runs on rigidly puritanical lines," Charles answered reasonably enough.

"Yes, but we need more than this. When he comes in, Malvolio's eyes should be offended by what he sees."

"Surely three drunken men singing bawdy songs is offensive enough?"

"No, no. We need something visual. The three should look in a way that somehow outrages his sen-sibilities. It is something they are wearing, or how they are wearing it."

"Well, they could have their doublets undone and drink spilled all over them."

"Yes, this is good, Charles, good."

"Oh." He was taken aback. It was the first time since they'd met that Alexandru Radulescu had de-scribed any of his ideas as "good."

"Doublets undone—yes, good, I like it. And with their doublets undone...what is it that Malvolio sees?"

"Well, their shirts...grubby linen, I sup-pose...though I'm not actually sure that it would be grubby. I mean, Sir Toby may be an old rake but—"

"No." The lines around the black eyes tightened, as they always did when the director produced another of the "radical ideas" for which he was so famed. "What Malvolio sees under their doublets," he pronounced triumphantly, "are T-shirts."

"T-shirts?" came the feeble echo from Charles Paris.

"Yes, T-shirts. They would offend his puritan sensibilities I think, no?"

"Yes, they probably would. They'd also confuse him totally, I would imagine, since they weren't due to be invented for another three hundred years."

But, as ever when Alexandru Radulescu was following the thread of a new idea, he did not even hear counterarguments. "Excellent, good, yes. They are wearing T-shirts that would offend his puritanism. 'Legalize cannabis,' this would be a good one, I think."

"What?"

"Or 'Fuck the Pope.'… You can, I think, get T-shirts that say 'Fuck the Pope.'"

"Except it's a sentiment that Malvolio, as a puritan, would probably agree with, anyway," Charles couldn't help objecting.

"Good point, good point…so we won't have that one. 'Guns N' Roses'!"

"What?"

"You will have a 'Guns N' Roses' T-shirt under your doublet. That would certainly offend Malvolio."

"But, Alexandru…"

It was hopeless. Once the director had got the bit

between his teeth, nothing could stop him galloping over the horizon with his latest brain wave. Anachronisms began to erupt all over the play.

Viola, as Cesario, was taken out of doublet and hose and put into doublet and jeans, "to stress the refreshing informality of her approach to Olivia." Antonio was to wear a leather, peaked cap and biker's jacket over his puff-sleeved shirt and slashed hose, "to emphasize the gay thing." Benzo Ritter and the First Officer were armed with pistols in holsters "so that the audience realizes the real threat to Antonio." Feste, in his disguise as the parson Sir Topas, was given a clerical dog-collar and, of all things, a laptop computer on which to note down Malvolio's answers to his questions. Maria, when flashing a leg, would reveal sexy stockings and suspender belt.

It was only with reluctance that Alexandru Radulescu was dissuaded from having Orsino deliver his opening "If music be the food of love..." while listening to a Walkman.

IT WAS THE END of their last day's rehearsal in London, a Saturday. Sunday off, then all reassembling at Chailey Ferrars on Monday morning for a no doubt agonizing sequence of technicals and dress rehearsals before the Tuesday-night opening. They'd done a full dress run in the rehearsal room that day, and the general view was that it had gone very well.

Charles Paris did not share that general view. Chad Pearson had been encouraged to put all kinds of new business into his performance as Sir Andrew Aguecheek, and the whole balance between the dominant, manipulative Sir Toby and his petulant dupe had been lost. Alexandru Radulescu's policy of "challenging accepted stereotypes" had resulted in something merely eccentric.

The homosexual kiss had not yet been written in, but it had already been discussed. Charles had the ominous feeling that its inclusion was only a matter of time. And no doubt if, when the moment arose, he objected, he would once again be branded as racist. And homophobic. People of Charles's age found mere survival tricky, as bulls in the china shop of modern political correctness.

The cast dispersed quickly at the end of the run. Benzo Ritter was once again left droopy like a rejected spaniel, as Sally Luther shot off with only the most perfunctory of good-byes. But everyone was in a hurry. Once they moved to Great Wensham, the three-month tour had effectively started. Most of them had sex lives to put on hold or partners to placate.

Charles Paris, left wondering whether his partner could ever be placated again—and indeed even whether the word *partner* was still appropriate—lingered. He'd persuaded Frances to let him take her out for dinner that evening, but he didn't approach the encounter with enthusiasm.

Then on the Sunday she was going to visit their daughter, Juliet, husband Miles, and three grandchildren. Charles had been assured that he'd be welcome too, but somehow didn't see himself going. So he recognized he was close to some sort of good-bye to Frances.

How permanent a good-bye he couldn't be sure, but he didn't feel optimistic. He tried to pinpoint the moment during the last few weeks when things had started to go wrong. It really all dated from Gavin Scholes's illness. Uncertainty over the change of director had got Charles drinking again, and the drinking had once again been a contributory factor to his soured relations with Frances.

As he moved morosely toward the green room to pick up his bag, the decision formed in Charles's mind to stop for a couple of large Bell's on his way back to the flat. He'd a feeling he might need bracing for the evening ahead.

He was about to enter when he heard voices from inside the green room. He wouldn't have stopped if he hadn't heard a mention of his name. In the event, he loitered out of sight and listened.

There was no problem identifying the speakers. Charles immediately recognized the dark, guttural sounds of Vasile Bogdan and the lighter West Indian lilt of Chad Pearson.

"No, Charles Paris is in a different play from the rest of us," said Vasile.

"Well, he's a traditional kind of actor," Chad Pearson offered in mitigation. He had an exceptionally amiable disposition; it really hurt him to think ill of anyone.

"Yes, but he's getting in the way of what Alex is trying to do. His scenes just aren't working."

"He'll be fine. Everything'll shake down when we get into the run." Chad Pearson still didn't want the boat rocked. "It's too late for anything to be done about it, anyway."

"Is it?"

"What do you mean?"

"Well, you're playing Sir Andrew Aguecheek, aren't you?"

"Sorry, Vasile? I'm not with you...?"

"Until last week Sir Andrew Aguecheek was being played by another actor who didn't fit into Alex's scheme of things. Then fortunately he got ill, and now you're playing the part."

"Yeah, well, I feel rotten about poor old John B., but...it's an ill wind."

"Yes.... Wouldn't it be great if another ill wind could just...blow away Charles Paris?"

"But if that happened, who'd play Sir Toby Belch?"

"I could do it," Vasile Bogdan replied. "I'd do it bloody well, actually...if only Charles Paris wasn't around." There was a silence. "Still, better be moving."

Charles backed away from the green-room door and tried to look as if he were fascinated by a copy of the *Daily Mail* somebody had left lying about. But he knew it was a bad performance, and the look Vasile Bogdan gave him in passing only confirmed that.

Vasile knew his words had been overheard. In fact, Charles got the distinct impression Vasile had spoken as he had only because he *knew* Charles was listening.

His words had been a deliberate threat.

"IT'S JUST the predictability, Charles."

They were in a Hampstead bistro they'd often been to before. Soon Charles would feel the need to order a second bottle of wine. On previous occasions they'd happily knocked back two and then moved on to the Armagnac. But this evening Frances was only sipping at her glass. The order for a second bottle was likely to prompt a sigh and a raised eyebrow.

"How can you call me predictable? You can accuse me of a lot of things, Frances, but not that. We make an arrangement—I may turn up, I may not turn up. I say I'll call you tomorrow, and you may not hear from me for three months. That's the secret of my great appeal—you never know where you are with me."

Had he looked into her face earlier, Charles might not have completed the full speech. He'd clearly chosen the wrong tack. Lighthearted irony was not what the occasion demanded. Frances shook her head wearily and pushed the hair back out of her eyes.

"It's the predictability of your unpredictability I'm talking about, Charles. That's what gets me down. I mean, how many new dawns am I expected to greet? How many times am I supposed to believe in you as a born-again dutiful husband? How many good intentions am I meant to listen to, while all the time I hear the Hell Paving Company truck revving away in the background?"

Charles grinned at the conceit, then looked serious.

"Look, I do mean everything I say at the moment I say it."

"Well, thanks. That's a lot of help, isn't it? I'm sure a goldfish is surprised every time it does a circuit of its bowl and sees the same bunch of weed."

"What's that meant to mean?"

"That, okay, maybe you do mean everything you say at the moment you say it, but that doesn't mean you're always saying it to the same person."

He looked puzzled, so she spelled it out for him. "Charles, it's very difficult for me to believe anything you say to me—anything caring, anything about loving me, for instance—when I know the next day, or the day before, you'll either say or have said exactly the same words to someone else."

"Oh, Frances, that was ages ago. I've grown out of all that. I now know what I want in life, and it's you."

"So all those other women...?"

"There never were that many...and none who really meant anything to me."

"Must've been nice for them to know that, mustn't it?"

"Frances... You should never worry about me and other women."

"I agree. And generally speaking, I've found the best way of not worrying about them is to close my mind to the fact of their existence. Which is a lot easier to do when I'm not being constantly reminded of the fact of *your* existence."

"You mean when I'm not around?"

"In a word, yes," she replied brutally.

"But, Frances..." He knew he was sounding pathetic. He didn't want to sound pathetic, but that was how the words came out. "There's still so much between us."

"Is there? Listen, Charles, what you don't realize is that things change. I change. You think I'm just the same person. You go away, have an affair, and when you get bored with it or she gets bored with it, you think you can come bouncing back and I will still be exactly where you left me. Life doesn't work like that. Every pain takes its toll. Each time you've hurt me it's left a mark—and strengthened my defenses against you, against the same things happening again. I'm a lot stronger than I was when you first walked out, Charles."

"I know. That's part of your appeal for me."

"I haven't built up that strength for *your* benefit. Rather the reverse, actually. I've built it up for me, so that I've got the strength to lead my own life, on my own, which is what I was doing, quite cheerfully, until, a month ago, you shambled back into it."

"You were pleased to see me. You welcomed me."

"Yes, you're right. I did manage to forget about the past. I managed to forget the predictability. Once again I deluded myself that, this time, it'd all be different."

"And it has been."

"Has it, Charles? Oh, the first two weeks were fine, yes, I agree. But would you say the last two have been very different from the way it always was?"

"Well..." Charles looked away from her and, as he did so, caught the eye of a passing waiter. He lifted up the empty wine bottle. "Could we have another one of these, please?"

ON THE LANDING back at the flat, he put his arms round her. "Good night," Frances said. "As you know, I'm going to Juliet's tomorrow. I don't suppose you...?"

He shook his head.

"No, no, I thought not. Well, Charles, I hope everything goes well at Great Wensham."

"Mm. Thanks." He'd had plans for organizing first-night tickets for her and... But it all seemed a bit pointless now.

"And keep in touch, eh, Charles?"

"But not too much in touch?"

She looked up and the pain in her eyes burnt into him.

He still had his arms around her. He really wanted her. Maybe, if they made love, it'd sort everything out.

He squeezed her tighter. "Frances..."

"What?"

What indeed? There was no point in trying to make love to her if she didn't want to. It just wasn't an act of sex he wanted; it was the coincidence of two people who really wanted to have sex with each other.

Slowly he released his hold. "I'll ring...you know, keep you up-to-date with how things're going."

"Mm." The disbelief in her monosyllable was not quite overt. "Take care, Charles."

She leaned forward and gave him a soft peck on the

cheek. Then her bedroom door opened and closed, and she was gone.

Charles Paris went through into the sitting room and poured himself a large Bell's.

THIRTEEN

HE WOKE IN the spare bed, tired and headachy. The stableyard taste in his mouth suggested he'd passed out before cleaning his teeth the night before. Nausea lurked in the cobwebs at the bottom of his throat. Why did he do it? Convivial drinking with other people was at least fun while it was happening; drinking alone was nothing more nor less than self-punishment.

There was an empty stillness in the flat. He glanced at his watch. After ten. God knows what time he'd fallen into bed. He didn't want to move, but his straining bladder insisted.

Being upright didn't help the headache. In the bathroom he peed copiously, sluiced his face in water, and cleaned his teeth. The mint wasn't strong enough to swamp the other taste in his mouth.

The door to Frances's bedroom was closed. He knew she wasn't there, but still tapped on it before entering. The room seemed almost clinically neat, the edges of the bedspread regulated into neat parallels.

The whole place smelled of Frances. A strong whiff of her favorite perfume in the air suggested she might only just have left. Maybe the closing of the flat's front door was what had woken Charles.

He sat on the bed, hunched in misery. This time he really had screwed up. Frances had given him a chance, and he'd blown it. What was more, it felt ominously like a last chance. They'd made no plans to meet again.

He could have stayed there, marooned in self-pity all day, but he forced himself to stand up. His weight had left a semicircular indentation on the bedspread. He smoothed it out. The bed was once again a rigid rectangle, as if Charles Paris had never been there at all.

He got dressed and tried to drink some coffee, but gagged on it. Savagely, he took a long swig straight from the Bell's bottle, recognizing as he did it—and almost reveling in—his self-destructive stupidity.

Then he went to the phone and rang Gavin Scholes.

WHEN HE REACHED the neat, terraced house in Dulwich, Charles was surprised to discover that Gavin had developed a new wife. The former one had walked out after many years in Warminster because, although he lived only a mile from his work, her husband was never home. Gavin was so obsessed with the Pinero Theatre that he gave little sign of having noticed his first wife's departure.

The new one was on the verge of walking out too when Charles arrived. Only temporarily, though her tone of voice implied a more permanent separation was not out of the question.

"Sorry to appear inhospitable," she said, "but I have so few opportunities to get out at the moment that I have to snatch every one that comes along."

"You mean Gavin's too ill to be left on his own?"

"No. I mean that Gavin *thinks* he's too ill to be left on his own—which, in terms of how much freedom it gives me, comes to the same thing."

"Ah."

"He's in the sitting room—through there. I'm going for a walk in the park. Can you stay for an hour? I won't be longer than that, I promise. But please don't leave him till I come back."

Through her brusqueness, a genuine anxiety showed. However much she tried to dismiss Gavin's illness as hypochondria, deep down she was worried about him.

The director was certainly doing the full invalid performance. Dressed in pajamas and dressing gown, he sat in an armchair facing French windows that opened onto a punctiliously regimented garden. (That must be the new wife's doing; Charles couldn't imagine Gavin Scholes showing interest in any activity outside the theatre.)

Beside the patient, Sunday papers lay unopened on a table, which also bore a bottle of Lucozade and a basket of grapes. The attention to detail was maintained, in spite of the summer weather, by a rug over Gavin's knees. The room even contrived to carry a hint of hospital disinfectant.

"How're you doing?" asked Charles.

It was an incautious, though probably unavoidable, question. Whatever the reality of Gavin Scholes's illness, he was certainly obsessed by it, and Charles did not escape the blow-by-blow, or perhaps twinge-by-twinge, account of every last bowel movement.

Gavin finally drew breath long enough for Charles to ask, ''And what does your doctor reckon it is?''

The director shrugged. ''Bloody hopeless, doctors these days. You never catch one committing himself to an actual opinion. It could be this, it could be that, better have some more tests... Never get a straight answer out of them.''

''So you've had tests, have you?''

''Oh, yes.'' Gavin spoke as a connoisseur of tests. Clearly his health was the one subject that could threaten the exclusivity of his obsession with theatre.

''And have they found anything?''

He shook his head. ''Nothing definite as yet. They can see I'm ill, but none of them has a clue what it is. My GP even had the nerve to suggest the whole thing was psychosomatic.''

''Well, you have always been a bit prone to that sort of thing, haven't you?''

''What do you mean?'' Gavin was incensed by Charles's casting doubt on the authenticity of his precious symptoms.

''I mean you have suffered from irritable bowel syndrome in the past...you know, when you've been stressed or—''

''Irritable bowel syndrome is not a psychosomatic disorder,'' said Gavin, still offended by the suggestion. ''It's a genuine illness—and absolutely crippling for those who have it. I've been a sufferer for years.'' Then, to compound his martyrdom, he added, ''Mind you, what I've got now is considerably more serious than that.''

"Hm." Time to move the conversation away from Gavin's cherished symptoms and get on with a bit of investigation. "There hasn't at any point been a suggestion that it might have been something you ate?"

"Something I ate?"

"Yes. That caused you to be ill?"

"What, just food poisoning?" Gavin's tone dismissed the unworthy idea. "No, what I've got is much more serious than that. Anyway, if it was food poisoning, I'd have recovered by now."

"It depends what you'd been poisoned with."

"And I'm sure some of the tests would have picked it up if that's all it was."

"That may not have been what the tests were looking for."

"I don't know why you're harping on about this, Charles."

"I was just thinking...the day before you were taken ill, we'd done the photo call and press conference at Chailey Ferrars..."

"Yes. So?"

"Well, I was just wondering whether you might have been poisoned by something you ate from the buffet."

"Why? Did other people who were there get ill?"

"No."

"Then why should I have done? What am I supposed to have eaten that caused this, anyway?"

"I did notice you have a mushroom tartlet." As he said them, Charles realized how stupid his words sounded.

"Yes, I remember it. Why should that have made me ill?"

"Well, suppose the tart had not been made with mushrooms, but with some other form of poisonous fungi..."

Gavin Scholes looked at Charles in blank amazement. "Why? Why on earth should it have been?"

"I've just been thinking...the timing was odd. You get ill—you can't continue directing *Twelfth Night*."

"Yes." Suddenly Gavin understood what Charles was hinting at. "Are you suggesting that I was deliberately poisoned to get me out of the way?"

"That's exactly what I'm suggesting."

"Well, it's absolute, total rubbish." The invalid was very offended now. An insinuation of foul play was the ultimate insult to his precious symptoms. "I am genuinely ill, Charles, not the victim of some crazed poisoner. Honestly, you really mustn't let your imagination run away with you like this."

"No. No. Sorry."

ASKING GAVIN SCHOLES the questions Charles had come to Dulwich to ask did not prove easy. The director had become highly skilled at finding in any unrelated sentence a cue for further medical reminiscence. If Charles mentioned Sir Toby Belch, Gavin was prompted to details of his wind problem. Talk of the rehearsal room unearthed the coincidence that the laboratory to which his stool sample had been sent was also in Willesden. And even the word *production* was picked up when Gavin said, "Goodness, you've no idea the production they made of giving me my barium enema.''

Charles noted that Gavin had developed the true hypochondriac's possessiveness. Everything was "my." Not just "*my* barium enema," but also "*my* consultant," "*my* enterologist," "*my* proctologist," and so on. Charles got the feeling Gavin would only be truly happy when he was qualified to talk about "*my* operation." He began to see why the new wife seized every opportunity to get out of the house and away from the unending litany of medical minutiae.

What was striking, though, was that Gavin Scholes showed absolutely no interest in how *Twelfth Night* was going. While he had been in charge, the play had consumed his every waking thought; now it was out of his hands, he might never have had anything to do with the show. He did not even express regret at the illness that had taken him away from the production. Why should he? That illness had provided him with a subject of much more consuming interest than anything the theatre could offer.

Gavin's medical monologue ensured that Charles had no problem staying an hour; indeed the promised time was almost up before he managed to shoehorn in the other questions he'd taken the trip to ask. And the only way he finally succeeded was by interrupting an account of catheterization with the words "Vasile Bogdan!"

The surprise was sufficient for Gavin Scholes to stop in his tracks and say, "What?"

"I wanted to ask you something about Vasile Bogdan."

"Oh. Why?"

"I just wondered how he came to be in the company."

"Well, he's a good actor, isn't he?"

"Yes, but you hadn't worked with him before, had you?"

"No. I don't only work with people I've worked with before, you know, Charles." Gavin sounded aggrieved, though the implied criticism had been justified. He employed only actors he had worked with before or actors recommended by actors he had worked with before.

Which was why Charles next asked, "So who recommended Vasile to you?"

"He auditioned for me," Gavin replied, still a bit huffy at having his casting methods questioned.

"But someone must've suggested his name for you to audition him."

"I'd heard good reports of him. I looked him up in *Spotlight*, thought he had an interesting face, so I asked him to come along for an interview."

"But who—?"

"It's not as if he was completely unknown, Charles. He'd got quite a track record for good work. Even West End...well, that is to say, the Old Vic."

"What'd he done at the Old Vic?"

"Oh, nothing very big, but apparently he was good."

"You didn't see him?"

"No." A defensive look came into Gavin's eyes. "When you're busy directing, it's difficult to get to see every show that opens, you know."

"Sure." The director was notorious for never going to see any productions other than his own. "So what was the play Vasile was in?"

"*She Stoops to Conquer.* Just played one of Tony Lumpkin's drinking cronies, I think, but, as I said, supposed to be very good."

"That was the production Alexandru Radulescu did, wasn't it? Another of his 'revisualization' jobs."

Gavin shrugged. "Don't know. As I said, I didn't see it."

"So who was it who recommended you should audition Vasile? Was it someone who you'd already cast in *Twelfth Night?*"

"Yes. And I thought he sounded an interesting actor, so I saw him. I'm always on the lookout for new talent," Gavin lied.

Charles patiently repeated his question yet again. "So who was it who first mentioned Vasile's name to you?"

"Russ Lavery. You know, Russ told me he'd once been taken ill with abdominal pains. Only an appendix in his case, obviously not as serious as what I've got. In fact, my consultant was only saying to me a couple of days ago, 'If only we were dealing with something as straightforward as an appendix, we'd know where we stood. As it is, Mr. Scholes, your case has got me completely baffled. I wouldn't be surprised if you get written up in *The Lancet*, you know. You have an extraordinarily interesting...' "

And Gavin Scholes was back on track. Charles extricated himself with difficulty once the new wife had returned. And as he left, he felt more than a little sympathy for the look of resigned panic he saw in her eyes.

FOURTEEN

THE GREAT Wensham Festival had been started ten years previously, on a great wave of local enthusiasm. Like many such enterprises, it had been the brainchild of one determined and charismatic individual, a local woman who, having brought up a family, was looking for something different to consume her inexhaustible energy. The complexity of setting up an arts festival was exactly the sort of challenge she relished. By a mixture of charm, bullying, cajolery, and sheer bloody-mindedness, she set up the whole thing from a standing start within a year.

And local people still talked back to the first Great Wensham Festival. There had been a raw excitement about it, the novelty of multifarious plays, concerts, and exhibitions all being crammed into one week, a sense of danger. For seven days Great Wensham had ceased to be another boring little Hertfordshire town and had come to life. Local people were caught up in the communal fervor. Many volunteered to help make the Festival happen; many more flocked to the scattered venues, and almost all of the artistic events were sold-out.

Buoyed up by that success, the second year's Festival was even more exciting. The one week was extended to ten days. The program was larger and more varied; more local buildings were commandeered as venues; the recruitment of volunteers grew ever wider. Famous names were engaged to appear; national reviewers came to write about the shows. The town filled with cultural tourists; business boomed. The summer Festival became established as a highspot in the Great Wensham social calendar.

That was in the early seventies, when the idea of a local arts festival was original. But over the years every tin-pot town in the country started to develop its own comparable event. Artistes and agents grew cannier; the network of festivals became just another booking circuit. As it had been in the days of music hall, the same performers took the same performances round the country, often unaware that their appearance was as part of a "festival." It all became predictable and not a little dull.

For Great Wensham, the rot set in when the prime mover behind the early successes left the area. Her marriage broke up—due in no small measure to the pressures of running the Festival—and she moved away. Recognizing that the initial thrill of that kind of festival had gone forever, she developed a new and successful career as a concert agent.

Without her dynamism, the Great Wensham Festival might have been expected to shrivel away to nothing. But by then the committees had taken over. The Great Wensham Festival Society had been born, representing the great and the good of the area. They rather liked the idea of their town continuing to host a nice, safe, contained ten-day festival. The shopkeepers were particularly keen.

By this time a new breed had appeared in the arts world—the professional festival administrator—and it was to one of these that the Great Wensham Festival Society had turned in their hour of need. Julian Roxborough-Smith was already running the Barmington Festival with apparent success; inviting him to take over Great Wensham was a logical step.

And so, with Moira Handley at his side to do all the actual work, Julian Roxborough-Smith started his act of juggling artistes between the two events. Since he also acted as agent for quite a few of the performers involved, he did rather well out of the arrangement.

The Great Wensham Festival continued to happen every summer. But the excitement, the energy, the danger, had gone.

THE *TWELFTH NIGHT* tech run at Chailey Ferrars had been scheduled to start at eleven on Monday morning. The obvious objection that the effects of the lights could not be judged in daylight was supposed to have been countered by a light-plotting session—without the cast—on Sunday evening.

The theory was that during the dress rehearsal, scheduled as per performance for seven-fifteen on Monday, levels could be tweaked, spots repositioned, and the lighting plot generally adjusted. Recognizing that this might be inadequate provision, the cast, after consultation with the Equity representative, had been asked to hold themselves in readiness for a couple of hours' fine-tuning on the lights after the dress rehearsal ended, which should be around ten-thirty.

The Asphodel production of *Twelfth Night* did not actually run three and a quarter hours. The playing time was just over two and a half, but a forty-five-minute interval was mandatory at Great Wensham, so that the locals could enjoy what they all referred to as "a Glyndbourne-style picnic."

Alexandru Radulescu had stamped his little foot a lot when he heard this demand, insisting that "my productions are about ensemble work and my cast cannot be expected to keep their concentration with a three-quarters-of-an-hour gap in the middle of the play."

But to no avail. Going to see the Great Wensham Festival Shakespeare was a social rather than an artistic event for the local audience. In fact, most of them would have preferred to watch a brass band and fireworks, but if they couldn't have that, Shakespeare'd have to do. Whatever the entertainment offered, the demands of their picnics took unquestioned priority. They made a big deal of the occasion. Some parties would arrive hours before the performance started, weighed down with folding tables, chairs, hampers, linen, cut glass, and even, in a few cases, candelabra.

The three-quarters-of-an-hour interval was incorporated, "to give us a bit of a time buffer," into the proposed schedule of technical and dress rehearsals for *Twelfth Night*. However, and it seems there's always a "however" in the theatre where tech runs are concerned, everything got hopelessly behind.

The fault lay not with Asphodel. Their backstage team was compact and highly efficient. The production company knew the pressures of touring and accordingly hired the best staff available. They all arrived at the agreed time on the Sunday afternoon, ready to erect *Twelfth Night*'s cunningly minimalist set on the stage, and to adjust the lights in the towers and gantries that surrounded it.

But when they got to Chailey Ferrars, there was no stage on which to erect the set. The scaffolding towers and gantries were in place. So was the metal load-bearing shell that covered the natural grassy mound; but the acting area, the boarding that should have been fixed onto this structure, was absent.

The problem was one of demarcation. Though the scaffolding was supplied and erected by outside contractors, construction of the staging was the responsibility of Festival volunteers. In previous years this group had been organized and coordinated by Moira Handley, whose judicious mix of bullying and flattery had built up a dedicated band of recidivists. Every year when reapproached about helping with the Festival, they all began by saying, "No way, never again." Every year they relented and, by the final event, had built up a tightly knit community with its own jargon and camaraderie. Many of them, in spite of the mandatory grumbles, took their annual holiday over the Festival period and regarded it as the highspot of their year.

However—another "however"—during the run-up to the current Festival, Julian Roxborough-Smith had piled yet another duty he should have undertaken himself onto the long-suffering shoulders of Moira Handley. He had asked her to organize the guest list for one of the final Festival events, the all-important Sponsors' Dinner and Chamber Concert, and Moira, in a rare moment of complaint, had objected that she really had far too much on her plate to take on anything else.

In a fit of pique at this unexpected resistance, Julian Roxborough-Smith had responded, "What've you got on your plate then?"

"Organizing the Festival volunteers, for a start."

"Oh, for heaven's sake, Moira. You do make heavy weather of everything." Which was possibly the most unjust criticism ever leveled.

"Julian, you've no idea how much time it takes—how many phone calls, chatting them all up, keeping them sweet, working out their rotas. You should try it sometime."

Stung by her tone, the Festival director had responded, "All right, I will. I will organize the volunteers this year. Then we'll see what you're making so much fuss about."

And indeed they did. Within a week Julian Roxborough-Smith had alienated the local roofing contractor who coordinated all the heavy-work volunteers. Then, by an injudicious display of temper, he'd reduced to tears the little old lady from the tobacconist who masterminded the box office. Incapable of admitting he was in the wrong, he reported to Moira that both of these essential supports to the Festival had resigned in fits of temperament.

He'd then issued invitations to virtually everyone he met to take over various Festival functions, which already had incumbents jealous of their precious little areas of responsibility. So more noses were put out of joint.

Finally, as the Festival approached, he produced a volunteers' rota so inflexible that it made Masonic ritual look impromptu. And all the time, whenever Moira inquired about how the volunteer organization was going, Julian Roxborough-Smith brushed her off with a dismissive, "Oh, for heaven's sake, woman, it's all in hand."

As a result, it was only the weekend before the Festival opened that Moira realized exactly how out of hand the whole organization was. The lack of staging at Chailey Ferrars was symptomatic of total chaos at all the Festival venues.

With superhuman energy—and at a time when all the other bubbling crises of the Festival were reaching boiling point—Moira threw herself into rebuilding the volunteer network. Some would never be reclaimed. The roofing contractor and the little old lady from the tobacconist had been alienated for good. Other reliable standbys, when not asked to participate, had either used up all their outstanding leave entitlement or actually gone away on holiday over the Festival period.

But Moira's skills of persuasion were exceptional, and by Monday morning, the day before the opening of the whole event, she had in place a workable infra-structure of volunteers.

Typically, Julian Roxborough-Smith did not thank her. In fact, if the subject of the chaos came up, he implied that it had been an error in Moira's organi-zation rather than his own.

The result of all this for the Asphodel *Twelfth Night* was that by the time the stage was in place, it was late on the Monday afternoon. With no time available for preparatory work on the lighting plot, the tech run be-gan at six forty-five. And it had been raining in Great Wensham since Saturday morning.

"WHAT'S A drunken man like, fool?" Olivia de-manded.

"Like a drowned man, a fool, and a madman," the Clown replied, "one draught above heat makes him a fool, the second mads him, and a third drowns him."

"Go thou and seek the crowner, and let him sit o' my coz; for he's in the third degree of drink: he's drowned."

Olivia's words could not have been more apt. The "coz" in question, Sir Toby Belch, was drowned in-deed. He would have given anything to be "in the third degree of drink" too, but Charles Paris hadn't touched a drop all day.

The rain had by now soaked through the thick char-coal velvet on his shoulders and was trickling down his back, between his stomach and its padding, every-where. His tights felt as though they had recently been painted onto his legs. Water still dripped incessantly off the brim of Sir Toby Belch's hat, from which the light gray feather dangled like a dead fledgling.

The canvas awning under which he stood offered no protection; it was as porous as a sieve. The allocated wing space was cramped and suddenly pitch-black after the brightness of the lights onstage. The trees surrounding the stage area were thought more important by the Chailey Ferrars trustees than the comfort of mere actors, whose entrances and exits had to be fitted around them. A kind of hessian tunnel led off from the stage toward the caravans that served as dressing rooms. Because of the trees and limited sight lines, the tunnel was narrow and actors had to press themselves against the walls to get offstage. Needless to say, the hessian was also wet.

Onstage was even wetter. Olivia blinked to keep the water out of her eyes. It dribbled off the ends of her straggled hair, sending little rivulets into her ample décolletage. The bell-tipped horns of the sitar-playing Feste's headdress drooped limply down around his ears.

Still, Charles had actually exited. Unless there was a sudden summons back, he would be free to go off and find some shelter. And a drink. He'd been very good all day, but now…hell, he needed one for medicinal purposes if nothing else.

"Hold it there for a moment, can we?" Alexandru Radulescu immediately dashed Charles's hopes. The director's voice came out of the darkness beyond the lights, which illuminated the cross-hatching of rain as it fell relentlessly onto the stage.

Charles peered out into the auditorium—though *field* might have been a better word to describe what he was looking at. Julian Roxborough-Smith's cock-up over the volunteers meant that the raked audience seating had not yet been delivered. The director, assistant director, and lighting designer huddled round a camping table in the middle of a space that would have served well as a location for a movie set in World War One trenches. A single sheet of polythene covered the three of them.

"Can we just go back to before Toby's exit?"

Shit.

"Positions for 'Lechery! I defy lechery...'" Charles shambled soggily back onstage. "And can you just hold that tableau while we adjust a couple of the parcans?" Alexandru's voice continued.

Oh, God. Moving the lights took forever. Someone would have to climb up one of the scaffolding towers and fiddle about with the angle of the beam until the lighting designer was satisfied. And unfortunately Asphodel's lighting designer was a perfectionist.

Charles, desperately willing the guy would settle for second, or even third, best, held his position. The damp was now creeping down his tights into his boots.

He sneaked a look at the watch he should by rights have taken off—and must remember to take off the following night. Alexandru Radulescu would probably applaud the anachronism, but Charles was determined not to give him the opportunity. He'd already secretly decided to ditch the Guns N' Roses T-shirt for the first night. He knew he'd get stick from the director afterward, but had promised himself he'd give at least one performance of Sir Toby Belch as Shakespeare had intended the part to be played.

The watch revealed it was nearly quarter past nine. God, and they'd only reached act 1, scene 5. Charles wished he'd gone straight off and got lost after his exit. By now he could be sitting somewhere dry with a large Bell's in his hand. But he knew his professionalism wouldn't let him do that; he'd be letting down the rest of the company. He had to wait only a few minutes, and then Sir Toby was off till act 2, scene 3.

The few minutes while the parcan was adjusted seemed more like hours, but eventually even the lighting designer was happy with the new setting. "Okay," Alexandru Radulescu's voice came through the rain. "Take it from after Sir Toby's exit."

"That mean I can go to the dressing room?" asked Charles.

"Yeah, yeah, sure. We're moving on."

The alacrity with which Sir Toby Belch moved to get offstage was ill-judged. Losing his footing on the wet boards, he skidded and fell hard on his bottom, prompting a trickle of uncharitable and disembodied laughter.

As he hurried off, pressed against the clammy walls of the hessian tunnel, Charles remembered he hadn't got anything to drink in his dressing room. Oh, shit, shit, and again shit.

He had had one of his misplaced attacks of righteousness that morning. Deciding that the booze had

been at least one of the causes of his cool parting from
Frances, he had made yet another vow to cut down.
He shouldn't be drinking on a rehearsal day, anyway.

So there was no comforting half-bottle of Bell's
tucked away in his jacket pocket in the caravan. (The
word *caravan* should perhaps be explained at this
point. In a theatrical context it might be expected to
describe a lavish "trailer" of the kind used by Hollywood stars on location. But no. The caravans parked
at the back of the stage at Chailey Ferrars were old,
green-stained, noisome, and damp. They were also
horrendously overcrowded. Three served the entire
Twelfth Night company. There was really only room
inside for the costumes, not the actors who were going
to put them on.)

Charles got the feeling that actors weren't very high
on the priority list for the organizers of the Great Wensham Festival. No one had greeted or welcomed the
Twelfth Night company when they arrived, and they
had been left to find their own way around the facil-
ities. It made them feel like strolling players, newly
come to the next barn they were due to storm.

He emerged from the end of the hessian tunnel, his
smooth-soled boots slithering in the mud. A solitary
working light hung in a tree spread a meager glimmer
over the scene. As he squelched off in the direction of
the caravans, Charles met someone coming toward
him. She was recognizably a woman, dressed in a navy
plastic anorak, which was sleek with rain. On the front
of the anorak was the white logo of the Great Wensham Festival. This was a fanciful combination of the

letters *G*, *W*, and *F* together with a shape that might
have been a waterfall or a scallop shell...or possibly
a unicorn. It was a piece of amateur artwork that explained instantly why major corporations will spend
millions to get a good logo.

She looked up into his face, and Charles recognized
Moira Handley, the Festival administrator.

"Oh, hi," he said.

"Charles Paris, isn't it?"

"You have a very good memory. We only met the
once at the press conference."

"Ah, maybe, but I've lived with you for nearly six
months." Seeing the puzzlement in his face, she
laughed. "Well, lived with your photograph."

"Oh." That was flattering. Charles Paris didn't
have that many fans, but all comers were welcome—
particularly when they were as attractive as Moira
Handley.

Her next words quickly disillusioned him. "It's one
of my jobs to get all the program copy together, so
my office is spilling over with photos and biogs."

"Ah. Right."

"God, you look drowned." She giggled. "How's it
going out there—the underwater *Twelfth Night*—star-
ring Esther Williams as Viola?"

"It is absolutely disgusting, but I don't see anyone
stopping it. If the show's to open tomorrow, we've
somehow got to get through this tech."

Moira nodded. She understood the imperatives of
the theatre. "Yes, if it's still like this tomorrow eve-

ning, we'll have to cancel, but the show has to be ready to go up.''

''Which means you can cancel a performance, but not the tech.''

''Exactly. I'm surprised you're doing it in costume, though.''

''Alexandru insisted. So did the lighting designer. Say you can't judge the overall effect unless everyone's dressed as they will be for the show.''

''Which is true, of course. What was the wardrobe mistress's reaction?''

''*Resigned* I think would be the word. I mean, the costumes have in theory been designed to cope with anything the elements can throw at them…. I just don't envy her trying to get everything dry for tomorrow night.''

''No.'' Moira lingered for a moment, as if about to move off. Then she said suddenly, ''Don't suppose you fancy a drink?''

''Those,'' Charles Paris replied, ''are the most wonderful words I've heard all year.''

FIFTEEN

CHARLES FOLLOWED HER. On the back of her navy anorak was printed in white: MUTUAL RELIABLE—FOR ALL YOUR FINANCIAL NEEDS—AND FOR THE GREAT WENSHAM FESTIVAL. Above the words was the professionally designed Mutual Reliable logo on which a large corporation had spent millions.

The Portacabin into which Moira led him was a few steps up in comfort from the dressing room caravans. One side was filled with desks on which piles of posters, handouts, and programs threatened to overwhelm the computers and telephones; on the walls, planning charts outlined elaborate schedules and rotas with colored strips and stickers; everywhere, papers bulged from the open drawers of battered metal filing cabinets.

On the other side of the room a dead sofa and a couple of terminally ill armchairs huddled round a table scattered with coffee jars, coffee cups, and coffee stains. The impression was one of controlled chaos.

"Is this the main administration office?" asked Charles.

"No, it's the Chailey Ferrars outpost. Main office is in the town, but so much needs doing out here, we have to have somewhere."

As she moved toward one of the filing cabinets, she

noticed a figure hunched in a chair, almost totally obscured by the mountain of paper on her desk.

"Oh, hi." A small, harassed face peered out over the debris. "Charles, did you meet our press officer?" asked Moira as she produced a bottle of red wine from a drawer.

"Yes. At the photo call. Hello...er...?" The name had gone completely.

"Pauline. Pauline Monkton. I recognized your costume from last time, anyway."

"Except it wasn't soaked through then."

"No."

Moira was now over at the grubby little sink, swilling out two glasses. Only two, Charles noticed. Pauline wasn't going to be invited to join them. Good.

"Surprised you're still here," the administrator observed. Was Charles being hypersensitive to detect a hint in the voice that perhaps the press officer should be on her way? Moira had stripped off her MUTUAL RELIABLE anorak, and he was aware of the firm outline of her body in its jeans and Guernsey sweater. Oh, dear. The old stage-manager syndrome was getting to him once again.

"Just came in to check the answerphone, Moira, see if any more of the press have said whether they're coming or not tomorrow. I mean, I've sent them all invitations with RSVP on, and none of them have even had the courtesy to ring back." Clearly Pauline Monkton's approach to publicity hadn't changed a lot in the last couple of weeks.

"We must know how many so we've got the right

number of seats reserved for them, Pauline. You'll
have to do a ring-round in the morning and check who
is actually coming."

"Oh, will I?" asked Pauline pathetically.

Moira was implacable. "Yes." She sat down on the
dead sofa and gestured for Charles to join her. She
slopped wine into the two glasses on the coffee table.
"Was there anything on the answerphone?"

"Something from... 'Saniserve' I think it was?"

"What?" The administrator was instantly alert.

"They said they'd tried to deliver at four this afternoon, but there was nobody around to let them in."

"Oh, shit!" Moira was furious. "Shit, shit, shit!"

"Is it important?" asked Pauline mildly.

"Yes, it is bloody important! Julian assured me he'd
got someone lined up to wait for them. Oh, bugger,
and there won't be anyone in their office now till the
morning."

"What were Saniserve trying to deliver?" asked
Charles cautiously.

"Only the most important thing in the entire operation. That without which the show cannot go ahead."
He looked at Moira quizzically as he sifted through
the possibilities. Extra lights? Backup generator? Fire
extinguishers?

"Portaloos," Moira announced. "We've got nine
hundred people booked in tomorrow night. At the moment there are no seats for them to sit on to watch
Twelfth Night, but that's okay—we could still go
ahead with the performance. But if we've got no toi-

lets for them to sit on, then we might as well forget the whole thing!''

"Oh.''

"Charles, you may think a festival like this is about the plays and the concerts and the performers who come together down here. It isn't. All it comes down to basically is seats and lavatories—that's the bottom line.''

He grinned at her inadvertent pun and was pleased that, through her annoyance, she could see the funny side too.

"But, if the worst comes to the worst, can't the audience use the loos inside the house?''

Moira's hands shot up to her face in mock-horror at the suggestion. "Inside *Chailey Ferrars?*''

"Uh-huh.''

"Charles, you could have the entire audience in the terminal stages of dysentery and the trustees would still not let them inside Chailey Ferrars out of opening hours—and unless they'd bought entry tickets.''

"Ah, dealing with dinosaurs here, are you?''

"Good heavens, no. They're not nearly as far advanced along the evolutionary track as dinosaurs.''

Charles chuckled. He liked Moira's cynical turn of phrase. And she was very tactile.

"Better be on your way, Pauline,'' Moira called across the room. "Big day tomorrow. You'll need your sleep.''

"Oh, I don't think I'll sleep a wink tonight,'' said the press officer, gathering together a sheaf of papers on her desk. "The thought of all those press people coming..."

"Or not coming," Moira suggested.

"Mm. I think I'd prefer that. If I actually knew that none of them was coming, then I could relax."

Once again Charles was forced to question whether Pauline Monkton had the right priorities for someone in the job she had been given.

"Still raining out there, is it, Moira?"

"Pissing down."

"I'd better take another of these." Pauline Monkton reached to a pile of polythene-bagged plastic anoraks. She split one out of its package and slipped it on, revealing the Mutual Reliable logo on the back.

"You seem to have plenty of those," Charles observed.

"Yes," Moira agreed. "Bye," she said in response to Pauline Monkton's muttered "See you in the morning." The press officer scuttled out into the dark, holding her hood up against the continuing downpour.

Moira Handley looked at Charles Paris and grinned. He grinned back as she picked up the conversation. "Bit ironic having all those anoraks, actually, since we've now lost Mutual Reliable as a sponsor."

"Really?"

"They'd supported the Festival last year—seemed all set to do it again—then suddenly backed out three months ago. Needless to say, just after we'd had the preliminary program printed—with their name all over everything."

"Why'd they back out?"

Moira Handley spread out her hands and made a little plosive. "Pff. Didn't reckon they were getting enough out of it. Sponsorship's not undiluted, altruistic charity, you know. All sponsors want a quid pro quo. It was decided at Mutual Reliable that they weren't getting their quid—or is it their quo?—out of the Great Wensham Festival, so…" She shrugged. "Now they're sponsoring a golf tournament instead."

"Oh?"

"The majority of their corporate clients would much rather get hopelessly pissed in a marquee at a golf club than have to sit through three hours of Shakespeare."

"So who's sponsoring the Festival now?"

Moira shrugged. "A hotchpotch of local firms and…let's say anyone we can get our hands on. Anyone who'll stump up a few bob. And in the meantime we have to go round scratching Mutual Reliable logos off everything in sight—and trying to off-load the plastic anorak mountain." She gestured to the pile. "We're handing them out all over. You fancy one?"

"For the rest of the rehearsal, you bet. And Alexandru'd probably think it was great. He seems determined to get as many anachronisms into this production as possible."

"I don't detect a little hint of criticism there, do I, Charles Paris?"

"What? Heaven forbid." But he could tell she saw through his denial. "Anyway, even if the director sanctioned an entire production of *Twelfth Night* in

Mutual Reliable anoraks, I somehow don't think the lighting designer would allow it.''

''No.''

Charles still felt soggy, but better in the warmth of the Portacabin. The wine was slipping down a treat too. And he didn't think he was completely misreading the signals in Moira Handley's shrewd brown eyes.

He looked round the room. ''So this is your domain, eh?''

''Part of it. Won't be able to shift from here much till your show's opened tomorrow night.''

Charles listened to the rain drumming on the flat roof. ''If it *does* open tomorrow night. Don't suppose you've got nine hundred of those anoraks, have you—one for each member of the audience?''

'''Fraid not.'' She picked up from what she'd been saying before. ''So I'll be staying here tonight...''

''Will you?'' asked Charles foolishly.

''Mm.'' She offered him an enigmatic grin. ''More wine?''

''Please.''

After she'd filled the glasses, there was no doubt that she ended up closer to him on the dead sofa.

''You married, are you, Charles?''

The direct question gave him a straight choice. If he really meant what he kept telling himself about his need to get back with Frances, then he should say yes. To say no would show up the hollowness of all his fine protestations.

In the event, he replied, ''Well, still technically, but... How about you?''

A firm shake of the head. "Never appealed. The thought of committing myself to one man...the thought of only ever making love to one man for the rest of my life...well, not for me, I'm afraid." Slowly but definitely, she put her hand on Charles's knee. "The thought of making love to lots of different men, though...the thought of making love to any man I fancy...that I do find more attractive."

"Mm... Yes, it's a good philosophy that. Good approach to life, really," he agreed fatuously.

Moira gave another of her little shrugs. "Workable, anyway."

"Right." There could be no doubt about her signals now. Charles, rendered doubly cautious by the existing climate of political correctness surrounding all interpersonal relationships, still couldn't find any ambiguity in what she was saying.

He looked into her eyes. They were sharp and teasing, daring him to take action. His face moved toward hers.

Their lips were almost touching when they were stopped by an electronic crackling. It came from a field telephone on a desk.

A voice emerged through the bacon-sizzling sound. "Does anyone know where the hell Charles Paris is? He's needed on-stage *immediately!*"

SIXTEEN

HIS BOOT SOLES skidding in the mud, Charles Paris hurried back through the trees toward the stage. Rain still dripped obstinately from the branches and sheeted across the open spaces between. He wished he had taken one of the Mutual Reliable anoraks, after all.

As he had the thought, someone dressed in one came hurrying toward him. It was a woman; the thin working light caught on the water-shiny plastic outline of her breasts. Though the head was averted against the weather—or perhaps against him—Charles could see straggling blond hair flicker out from under the anorak's hood.

The woman said nothing to him, possibly hadn't even seen him, but turned abruptly away between the trees in the direction of the cast caravans.

Charles pressed forward, feeling an idiot. For him to have missed his cue was a serious black mark. A tech is hell for everyone, a major test of company patience, but it is the duty of all cast members to be on hand—or at least somewhere whence they can be quickly summoned—at all times. There are enough technical problems to slow the process down without lost actors screwing things up. Charles didn't anticipate a warm welcome when he made his belated entrance.

On top of that, he was feeling stupid about what had happened with Moira. He berated himself for the weakness of his will. She was attractive, she appeared to be amenable, even enthusiastic, but he still shouldn't have responded so easily. His sole aim in life should be to make it up with Frances, for God's sake.

Charles dived into the hessian tunnel that led to the stage. It seemed even narrower and clammier than it had before. He skidded to the wing area and almost cannoned into Sally Luther, dressed in her soggy Cesario costume. Her blond wig dangled in tendrils liked overcooked pasta.

"Oh, I'm so sorry, Sally."

"Where the hell have you been?"

"Got delayed." He popped his head out onto the stage and shouted, "Sorry, Alex! I'm here now!" then smartly popped back in before the director could start bawling him out.

Sally Luther moved onto the stage and shouted, "Can I get back to my dressing room now he's here, Alex?"

"No."

"Oh, for God's sake! We've already been doing this scene for half an hour."

"Sally, I'm sorry, but we need the bridge between the scenes, because we've got to do the lighting change and move the chairs. We'll have to go back on the end of your scene. Take it from 'O Time, thou must untangle this…' Oh, just a minute.'' He had been interrupted by the lighting designer. ''No, we've just got to reset a couple of the lanterns. Could be five minutes. Nobody leave the stage…and that includes you, Charles Paris, you unprofessional bastard!''

Charles was stung by the words. To be called unprofessional is the worst insult any actor can receive, particularly when he knows the aspersion is justified. He shrunk into the wings against the damp hessian as Sally Luther and Chad Pearson came offstage to join him.

''I wouldn't get too close to that if I was you,'' the actress advised.

''Mm?''

''There's a holly bush or something behind it. I was standing there a minute ago and I got quite a nasty prick through the hessian. Just in the fleshy bit of my thigh—really stung.''

''Oh. Right. Thanks.'' Charles moved farther away from the screening and saw that he was now directly in view of half the audience (assuming that the Chailey Ferrars *Twelfth Night* ever did have an audience, an idea which at that moment seemed a laughable fantasy). ''Tight on sight lines, isn't it?'' Charles observed as he shrank back into the wings.

''Okay, we're set!'' Alexandru Radulescu's voice bawled out from the darkness. ''Back to 'O Time, thou must untangle,' Sally. And make sure you're ready for your cue, Charles bloody Paris!''

Sally Luther ventured back into the downpour

to complete her soliloquy at the end of act 2, scene 2.

"'O Time, thou must untangle this, not I. It is too hard a knot for me t'untie.'"

Shaking her head wearily—and to the sound of doleful sitar music—she moved off into the wings where Sir Toby Belch and Sir Andrew Aguecheek waited. Charles had always thought it a clumsy bit of blocking from Alexandru Radulescu to have her exit the same way they were about to come on, but he didn't think this was the moment to raise the point.

"Thank God for that," Sally Luther muttered as she passed. "I'm not in the next scene." And she hurried off toward the "dressing rooms."

Charles Paris and Chad Pearson made their entrance and then had to wait in the rain for further adjustment of the lights. The *Twelfth Night* tech wound on its weary course. At the current rate, Charles reckoned they'd be lucky to finish before four in the morning.

And a wicked, but unsuppressible, thought inside him conjectured what kind of response a knock on the Portacabin door at four in the morning might get.

IN THE EVENT, he never found out. The tech was not allowed to run its full course.

In the middle of act 2, scene 4, Orsino had just asked Cesario, "'And what's her history?'"

Sally Luther replied, "'A blank, my lord: she never

told her love, but let concealment like a worm i' th'
bud feed on her—'''

Suddenly she clutched at her throat and started gagging. She fell down onto the wet stage.

After what seemed an age, an ambulance made it
across the muddy grounds of Chailey Ferrars to pick
up the invalid and take her to the local hospital.

And on the next morning's radio and television
news bulletins it was announced that Sally Luther was
dead.

SEVENTEEN

THE TECH HAD ended in chaos with less than a third of the play rehearsed, so there was no surprise to have a company call for ten o'clock the following morning, Tuesday, the day *Twelfth Night* was due to open. Few in the cast expected that opening to happen as scheduled.

Charles Paris had gone back to his digs and slept little. (Somehow, in the circumstances, knocking on the door of Moira's Portacabin had seemed inappropriate.) He made a point of getting back to Chailey Ferrars early in the morning.

The weather had miraculously changed. As if Sally Luther's death had been some ritual sacrifice to propitiate the rain gods, Tuesday dawned bright and clear. Underfoot remained muddy, but the growing warmth of the sun promised to dry out the sodden field.

Moira's prodigious organizational skills were paying off. As Charles arrived at nine-thirty, groups of men were bolting together the metal structure of a raked auditorium. Women and boys were unloading stacks of chairs from a drop-side truck. Already the front few rows were fixed in position. So the audience would have seats to sit on that evening—though whether there would be a show for them to watch was more doubtful.

At the back of the auditorium stood two Land Rovers towing large caravans with the name SANISERVE printed on their sides. Moira had sorted that out too. Not only would the audience have seats to sit on, they would also be able to relieve themselves. There was nothing to stop the first-night performance from going ahead—except its lack of a central character.

Charles Paris knew exactly what he needed to do. He went straight up onto the stage to the wings through which he had exited and entered the night before. In the daylight the tented area looked untidy and amateur. The hessian drapes hung damply down, but already, where the beams of the sun caught them, a thin steam was beginning to rise.

Charles tried to remember Sally's exact words. Something about being careful, not standing too close to the drapes...about a holly bush...about feeling something prick through...something stinging her upper thigh...

He probed gingerly along the soggy fabric hanging, but could feel nothing pressing through from behind. He went backstage to check. The hessian screen, shabbier from this side and supported on irregularly angled tent poles, stood proud from the surrounding trees and shrubs. There was no holly bush for Sally Luther to have leaned against.

Which meant that, if something had punctured her skin, it must have been pushed through the drape from the other side. And Charles Paris didn't find it fanciful to think that something might have been a syringe.

This was serious now. Gavin Scholes could possibly

have been struck down by a genuine illness. John B. Murgatroyd's attack might just conceivably have been accidental food poisoning. But Sally Luther was dead, and it seemed very likely that she had been murdered.

Charles kicked himself for not taking action earlier. If he'd voiced his suspicions, the poor girl's death might have been averted.

On the other hand, the familiar question arose of whom he should have voiced his suspicions *to*. Previous experience had taught Charles that the police have a distinctly skeptical attitude to intimations of murder—particularly when they come from members of the theatrical profession. That all actors are self-dramatizing, effete—and probably gay—seemed to be an enduring conviction amongst the British constabulary.

He would need unanswerably solid proof of wrong-doing before he could take his accusations to the proper authorities. And at the moment he had no proof at all, only vague suspicions and a few, inadequately connected, links of logic.

There was also his position in the company to consider. Charles Paris was already unpopular enough without starting to spray around accusations of murder. He needed to be extraordinarily certain of his facts before he challenged anyone. A misplaced allegation of serious criminality from one cast member to another could prove to be a very inauspicious opening to a three-month tour.

There was of course a strong chance that, if Sally Luther had been murdered, the police would soon be on to the case. A death as sudden as hers must inevitably demand a postmortem, and if its finding showed she had been injected with poison, then the *Twelfth Night* company would quickly be swamped by inquisitive police officers.

But if, for some reason, that didn't happen...

Charles had to find out more.

THE GREAT Wensham Festival officials had turned out in force for the ten-o'clock call onstage at Chailey Ferrars. The Festival director was there, along with Moira Handley and Pauline Monkton. Asphodel's "accountant" was also present, flanked by Alexandru Radulescu, the lighting designer, and the assistant director.

Alexandru was the most overtly irritated by Julian Roxborough-Smith's long-winded oration, tapping his hand crossly against his knee, anxious to be active.

"...a terrible tragedy, of the kind which I am glad to say is unprecedented in the history of the Great Wensham Festival. On behalf of the Festival Society, and of course of our sponsors, I will be sending appropriate condolences to Miss Luther's family."

The company, in the front rows of audience seating, were as impatient as their director. They wanted to know what decisions had been made, and they wanted to know as soon as possible. All were twitchy. Only Talya Northcott looked serene, as her mind formulated the dream that was about to come true: "Understudy Rises to Tragic Challenge—A Star Is Born!" Mummy would really enjoy telling her friends about that. The scrapbook would fill up very quickly.

"One point I should mention," Julian Roxborough-Smith ground on, "is that there are always people who feed on and try to benefit from disaster—I refer of course to the press—and it's not impossible that, after what's happened, Great Wensham will become the target of the tabloid hacks. The Chailey Ferrars staff will be doing their best to keep these scavengers out, but in the event that any of you are approached by journalists, I would ask you to say nothing, just address all inquiries through the Festival's press officer—"

Pauline Monkton squirmed at the thought of more limelight and responsibility.

"—who I am sure is better qualified to handle such inquiries than you are."

The panic in the press officer's eyes cast doubt on the truth of this assertion. "We've had lots of calls already, Julian," she whispered breathlessly, "and I really don't know what to say to them. I think, if I just leave the answerphone on, then they'll probably stop ringing after a time."

Annoyance tugged at the corner of the Festival director's mouth, but he was too professional to give his press officer a public dressing-down for wimpishness and general incompetence, so moved smoothly on.

"If, on the other hand, you are approached by the police—and I don't at this stage know whether there is likely to be any form of police investigation—I would obviously rely on you all to cooperate fully.

"However"—he sighed and adjusted his floppy bow tie—"with every setback, even one so terrible and shocking as this, the question that must follow on from tragedy is, Where do we go from here? I've just come from a meeting with your director and"—he clearly didn't know the name of the person to whom he gestured—"this gentleman from Asphodel Productions, at which meeting we discussed the various options which are open to us.

"While I support in principle the old adage that 'the show must go on,' I am sure that you will all agree the show should only go on if the performance is of a standard that will not do discredit to your own high professional standards. Now in this instance a variety of potential scenarios offer themselves to us if we—"

"Oh, for Christ's sake, get on with it!" Alexandru Radulescu's patience was exhausted. "We're incredibly pushed for time, and you're just wasting more of it with all this long-winded crap!"

Julian Roxborough-Smith was so unused to anyone speaking to him like this that he could only gape and straighten his bow tie. Charles noticed that her boss's discomfiture brought an irrepressible grin to Moira's lips. She'd enjoy seeing that kind of thing happen more often.

The Asphodel representative suavely interceded to cover up Alexandru's rudeness. "I'm sorry, Mr. Roxborough-Smith, we're all obviously under a lot of stress."

The Festival director was still too shocked to do more than mouth back, so the accountant slid quickly

on, "And Alex does of course have a point. Time is
of the essence, so I think...if it's all right with
you"—he didn't give Julian Roxborough-Smith time
to say whether it was or it wasn't—"I should hand
straight over to our director, so that he can put forward
to the cast his proposed solution to a current crisis, a
solution which, in keeping with most things Alex does,
is extremely *radical*."

Charles groaned inwardly as the small figure of the
director stepped forward. The black eyes gleamed with
fanatical zeal.

"Friends, fellow workers, fellow artistes," Alexandru Radulescu began. "In no way do I wish to di-
minish what has happened. It is a terrible thing. Sally
was one of us—we have lost her. At the proper time
we will mourn her properly. But, for now, my priority
must be *Twelfth Night*."

Why suddenly? Charles's cynical mind couldn't
help supplying the question. It never has been before.

"This is not just my priority—it is *our* priority. And
it is a priority which Sally, of all people, would have
respected. The show, as Julian has said, must go on.
The question is how soon it goes on. My proposal
is—that we open tonight as scheduled."

A collective gasp of astonishment rose from the
company. They were all troupers, but surely what their
director was suggesting was impossible.

Talya Northcott voiced the communal objection. As
understudy to Viola, she had more reason than most
to be anxious. "But, Alex, we just haven't got time.

I mean, I know the lines all right, but I'd have to go through all the blocking and—''

"Besides," the lighting designer chipped in, "we haven't done the tech on the second two-thirds of the show. We've only got the roughest kind of plotting done for that."

"You can continue plotting as we rehearse," Alexandru announced magisterially.

"But look, that'll be daylight. We won't be able to judge how the—"

"That is what we will do."

Alexandru did not raise his voice, but the words were a testament to the strength of the little man's personality. The lighting designer was silent as his director repeated, "We will open tonight, as scheduled."

"But don't you think that shows a lack of respect for Sally's memory—as if we don't think her death's important?"

This latest objection, from Benzo Ritter, was slapped down as firmly as the others. "I do not think so. She was an actress. She would understand. Tonight's performance will not be a disrespect to Sally Luther—it will be a tribute to Sally Luther."

Alexandru Radulescu knew he had everyone's attention and he played his scene to the full. "As I say, we will open tonight, as scheduled"—he turned to Talya Northcott—"but I am sorry, my dear, you will not be playing Viola."

Like Julian Roxborough-Smith before her, the girl was stunned into silence. She too mouthed hopelessly.

Charles felt sure she had already been on the phone to Mummy about her big break, and Mummy had already rung round all her family and friends. Some embarrassing calling back was going to be necessary.

"I have said before," Alexandru continued, "that what some people regard as problems, I see as positive creative opportunities. All through rehearsal we have been saying that *Twelfth Night* is Shakespeare's exploration of the potentialities of human sexuality—"

Charles's knee-jerk reaction—"No, it isn't!"—once again remained unspoken.

"—and a solution to our current problem which extends the range of this exploration occurred to me very early this morning. It will need some revised blocking towards the end of the play, but this is not insuperable. You see"—he turned again to the stricken Talya—"we already have someone in the company who is fully rehearsed in the part of Viola. Yes, my friends, we will open *Twelfth Night* tonight with the parts of Sebastian *and* Viola both being played by Russ Lavery!"

There was another gasp from the company, which quickly gave way to delighted applause. Charles Paris looked round the semicircle of faces to gauge reactions. Apart from Talya Northcott, who could not suppress her tears, Benzo Ritter seemed the only one downcast by the news, presumably because he still thought it betokened disrespect for his lost idol.

Vasile Bogdan and Tottie Roundwood were ecstatic in their appreciation for another stroke of Radulescu genius. Chad Pearson shook his head, chuckling at the audacity of the solution.

And on the face of Russ Lavery was an expression of unambiguous triumph.

EIGHTEEN

THE REST OF the day was a tribute to the organizational skills of Alexandru Radulescu. He started by rehearsing act 5, the only moment in the play when Viola and Sebastian, brother and sister, are onstage at the same time.

He must have been up all night devising the blocking for this confrontation. Inevitably it involved the use of a double. Talya Northcott, who had been cast for her physical likeness to the compact Sally Luther, was awarded this role (the nearest she was ever going to get to playing Viola), but all the lines were to be spoken by Russ Lavery. Mummy and the large party of family and friends she had conscripted for the first night were due for a disappointment.

In Alexandru's revised blocking, by ingenious use of the entrances and exits, by a lot of crossing behind the emblematic trees of the simple set, Viola and Sebastian appeared, reappeared, and changed roles as in some elaborate conjuring trick.

When the Duke, upstage of the identical pair who faced him, said in wonderment, "One face, one voice, one habit, and two persons, a natural perspective, that is and is not," few of the company would have disagreed with him. The director had created another moment of theatrical magic.

Even Charles Paris, who thought this new twist served only to push Shakespeare's play further out of true, could not help but be impressed.

Given the opportunity, Russ Lavery demonstrated what an exceptional actor he was. After the popular success of *Air-Sea Rescue,* in which he played an amiable but two-dimensional character, there had been a tendency in the profession to dismiss him as "very limited—plays the one part fine, but that's it." Russ Lavery's work on *Twelfth Night* that day refuted any such criticism.

As he had begun to in the experiments of rehearsal, he created two totally different characters for Sebastian and Viola. The physical likeness was obviously there; there were vocal similarities, though Viola's voice was lighter and more feminine; but he differentiated the two so subtly that throughout the play there was never any question which of the twins had just come onstage.

In most productions of *Twelfth Night,* much effort is expended to make two people of different sex—frequently also of different height, bulk, and coloring—look alike. In Russ Lavery's performance, or performances, the likeness could be taken for granted, and so he was able to emphasize the differences between the two characters.

For anyone who knew anything about the theatre, the development was fascinating to watch. Russ Lavery's performance as Viola had come on so much from the sketchy outline he had revealed in previous rehearsal exercises.

It was almost as if he had prepared for this moment, as if he had known he would be playing the part.

THE UNHOSPITABLE NATURE of the Chailey Ferrars trustees for once proved a benefit. During the day of rehearsal they kept the estate firmly shut, so that the horde of tabloid journalists, drawn to Great Wensham by Sally Luther's name and the whiff of potential scandal, was unable to get near the *Twelfth Night* company.

In fact, the only way they could get into Chailey Ferrars was by buying tickets for the evening's performance. This was good news for the box office and also had the beneficial side effect of introducing to Shakespeare people whose only previous contact with English literature had been "Gotcha!" "Pulpit Pooftahs!" and "Queen: It's Been a Bum Year!"

Because of the intense rehearsal pressure, the grounds were not to be opened to the public until six-thirty, three-quarters of an hour before the performance. This caused a great deal of disgruntled harrumphing from hamper-laden regulars, who could not understand why something as minor as getting the performance right should be allowed to abbreviate their picnicking time.

The change in the weather had been maintained. The weekend's downpours had left the Chailey Ferrars lawns glowing with health; the surface moisture had dried off and the worst of the mud crusted hard. The audience seating was in place, chairs joined together in the requisite manner and passed as safe by the fire officer. The Saniserve lavatories were fixed and plumbed, ready for the worst the bladders and bowels of Great Wensham could throw at them. Volunteers were in position behind the bars of the refreshment tent, from which the spicy aroma of mulled wine fought for dominance with onion soup. Outside, under an awning, charcoal glowed beneath the grills that would soon be busy cooking hamburgers.

In the patrons' and sponsors' marquees (behind which were special patrons' and sponsors' superloos that played music and sprayed perfume), uniformed waitresses waited to dispense food and alcohol—the sponsors' only tangible reward for putting money into the arts. By the entrance gates, program sellers and usherettes, wearing sashes with the appalling GWF logo on them, massed in readiness. Men in Mutual Reliable anoraks crisscrossed the auditorium, talking importantly into two-way radios.

Six-thirty arrived. Incredibly, the Asphodel company had just completed a full run of *Twelfth Night.* The new moves and business in act 5 had worked without a hitch. Alexandru Radulescu gave a very few notes, thanked the cast for all their hard work, and instructed them to "fuck the bastards rigid!"

The great and the good of Great Wensham, at that moment admitted through the gates of the car park into the Chailey Ferrars grounds, were unaware of this exhortation—which was probably just as well, because they were a very straitlaced bunch.

They hurried in, outpacing each other with their tables and hampers, desperate to secure the best pitches on the grassy slopes behind the seating. And they settled down to enjoy their picnics and "Which one is it this year? Oh, yes, *Twelfth Night.*"

THE BRITISH notoriously love underdogs, they love stories of plucky little Britishers triumphing against overwhelming odds, so the first performance of the Asphodel *Twelfth Night* started on a wave of goodwill. The Great Wensham audience might not know a great deal about Shakespeare, but they were good on television drama and sitcoms, so the news of Sally Luther's death had shocked them all. The fact that the person stepping into the breach—as they were informed by a printed slip handed out with their programs—was none other than Russ Lavery, who played Dr. Mick Hobson in *Air-Sea Rescue*, ensured the production a sympathetically partisan reception.

But it wasn't just a softened-up audience that made the show go so well that night. And it wasn't just the communal spirit-of-the-blitz, let's-do-a-good-one-for-poor-old-Sally spirit that lifted the company to new heights. Alexandru Radulescu's production actually worked.

All the apparent perversities of his interpretation were ironed out in actual performance. The seemingly unconnected sequence of theatrical moments developed its own rhythm and momentum, as if part of some meticulously prepared master plan. It still wasn't Shakespeare's *Twelfth Night,* but it was a fascinating theatrical experience.

What made it perfect for Great Wensham was that

the production was experimental without being impenetrable. Somehow the outline of the story remained intact, so the audience's attention was held throughout. The show manifested a kind of licensed *enfant terriblisme,* which would enable the great and good of Great Wensham to say at drinks parties, "Oh, I'm not against experimental theatre, you know. I mean, we saw that very radical reinterpretation of *Twelfth Night* at the Festival, and we enjoyed that a lot, didn't we, darling?"

Even the company member most opposed to Alexandru Radulescu's innovations, Charles Paris, was forced to concede that the evening worked as a piece of theatre. To his annoyance, he even found himself caught up in the impetus of the production. His performance as Sir Toby Belch shifted away from the traditional—in his view, "right"—way of playing the part toward the style Alexandru Radulescu had been trying to impose on him. A more than friendly relationship with Sir Andrew Aguecheek emerged—though it stopped short of the mooted homosexual kiss. And under his doublet Charles Paris did wear his Guns N' Roses T-shirt.

But the show's real triumph belonged undoubtedly to Russ Lavery. The improvement shown in the day's rehearsals was maintained through the evening. He must have been utterly exhausted, but an adrenaline high spurred him to ever greater achievement. The rest of the company was infinitely supportive of him, and when, at the end of the performance, he came forward to take his solo bow, they joined in the audience's ecstatic ovation.

Russ Lavery, glowing with realized ambition, bowed and bowed again. He'd "gone back to his theatrical roots" and grown from the experience. After his fourth solo bow, since the applause showed no signs of abating, he stretched out a hand into the wings and gestured the director to join him.

The tiny figure of Alexandru Radulescu bounced onstage and took Russ Lavery's hand. They bowed together, incandescent in their mutual triumph.

Then the actor stepped forward and, managing eventually to still the audience, announced, "Thank you very much, ladies and gentlemen. I'd just like to say, on behalf of the entire company and crew, that we dedicate tonight's performance to the memory of a great actress and a very dear friend—Sally Luther. We love you, Sally—and we did it for you!"

As Russ stepped modestly back, the audience erupted into an even more vigorous ovation. For them the evening had had everything—a sensational news story, a star familiar from television, an "understudy triumphs" backstage drama—all this overlaid with the righteous, self-justifying glow of having "seen some Shakespeare."

ALL OF THE company were invited by Julian Roxborough-Smith to have a postperformance drink in the patrons' marquee. After the traumas and hard work of the previous thirty-six hours, they had earned it.

Charles Paris, who hadn't touched a drop since the

wine he'd shared with Moira Handley in her Portacabin, eagerly seized a glass of red from the tray of a
passing waitress.

"It's refreshing to see a production which concep-
tualizes from an alternative learning base and challenges the diktats of traditional authoritors, isn't it?"

If he hadn't recognized her face, Charles would
have known instantly that the granny-spectacled
woman speaking to him was Carole Whittaker of
HAN.

"Er…well…yes," he hazarded.

"Radulescu has an almost postmodernist attitude to
the text qua text, synergizing a kind of input to Shakespeare whose outreach goes beyond the microcosm of
received and conformable educational data—don't you
agree?"

"You're not wrong."

"So his extrapolations from the atavistically pro-
tected corpus of words known conveniently as *Twelfth
Night* come to represent a parallel but diverse textual
statement."

Charles Paris almost thought he understood that bit.
"You mean he's created a *Twelfth Night* that is different from Shakespeare's *Twelfth Night?*"

"At the most primitive level, yes. But at the same
time a process of intertextualizing is at work, so that
not only the verbalization is transformed, but the received definition of the media-related categorization in
which the opus partakes is also challenged."

"Hm. Too right." Charles nodded. "Erm…will you
excuse me?"

Carole Whittaker seemed unworried by his abrupt departure and moved to share her thoughts with Sir Andrew Aquecheek. Charles would always treasure the image of growing puzzlement that spread across Chad Pearson's genial features.

Alexandru Radulescu was moving round the room, gathering plaudits and spreading congratulations. He came face-to-face with Charles and grinned. ''Coming better, yes? I was right about how Sir Toby should be played—no?''

''Well...'' To have agreed would have been total hypocrisy. In performance Charles might have come closer to Alexandru's views, but he still didn't believe the director was ''right.'' He salved his conscience by avoiding the direct question and making a general comment. ''Thought the whole thing went wonderfully well—congratulations.''

The conversation might have continued had Alexandru Radulescu not been swept away by Julian Roxborough-Smith to meet Great Wensham's mayor, ''who is also a past president of the Great Wensham Rotary Club.''

Charles found himself face-to-face with Moira Handley. She grinned, but he noticed the tight lines of tiredness around her eyes. ''Very good,'' she said. ''I gather it went very well.''

He experienced the little pang all actors feel at such moments. ''You mean you didn't see it?''

''Saw the first ten minutes and most of the last act. We have got other performances on, you know. I had to put in an appearance at a Bach piano recital and a one-man show about W. B. Yeats.''

"Ah.''

"Then tomorrow it's Palestrina in St. Michael's Church, a lecture on stained glass at the Community Centre, literary lunch at the Marlborougn Hotel, bagpipes in the town square, Mozart in the corn exchange, the Amateur Operatics' *Brigadoon*...a few other events I've forgotten...finishing with alternative stand-up in the Big Top.''

"Busy schedule.''

"You could say that.''

"Well, if you have time in that busy schedule for a quick drink at some point...?''

Moira Handley shook her head ruefully. "Don't see it, Charles.''

"Oh.''

"I think we had a moment, you know...but I think the moment's probably passed.''

"Mm. Probably.''

He might have been left standing there pathetic and awkward if Pauline Monkton hadn't bustled up. She was bubbling with enthusiasm and self-confidence.

"Well, talk about press coverage, eh?''

Moira turned her quizzical gaze on the press officer, but said nothing.

"Couldn't have been better. All the nationals here. I think the secret with publicity,'' Pauline Monkton confided knowingly, "is not to bother about the RSVPs. Oh, yes, put them on the invitations, by all means, but if nobody replies, don't worry about it.

Doesn't mean they're not coming. Oh, no, publicity is about targeting the right individuals. Get the right press list, distribute invitations to the right people, and they'll come, no problem. Even spread it among their fellow journalists. Do you know''—her voice dropped to an awed tone—''there are press here tonight who I *didn't even invite.*'' She nodded complacently. ''Shows they got the message this was a first night that just shouldn't be missed.''

Charles and Moira exchanged looks, and he could tell they shared the same thought. The press presence at Great Wensham that evening had nothing to do with Pauline Monkton's strategy—with or without RSVPs. It was prompted entirely by the news of Sally Luther's death. But neither of them would be so cruel as to tell the press officer that.

Moira was summoned away to sort out some other cock-up over the volunteers, another task that Julian Roxborough-Smith had assured her he had ''completely in hand.'' Charles, left on his own, scooped up another glass of wine from a waitress's tray and looked around the scene.

It was really remarkable how little Sally Luther's death had impacted on the *Twelfth Night* company. Sure, at that moment they were all caught up in the communal euphoria of having got the show on against the odds, but he'd have expected a little more introspection. Instead, it seemed as though Russ Lavery's formal acknowledgment of the death had closed the subject. Sally Luther need never be thought about again.

The only person who still seemed affected by her absence was Benzo Ritter. The boy's face looked stressed, but even he was perking up. A few more drinks and he too would be able to forget his infatuation—at least for a little while.

Charles Paris wondered whether Sally Luther's murderer was in the marquee at that moment. If his theory was right, if her death had been one in a sequence of poisonings, then that was likely.

The perpetrator must have been present at the Chailey Ferrars press conference after which Gavin Scholes had become ill, in the Indian restaurant that did it for John B. Murgatroyd, and around the stage during the *Twelfth Night* tech the previous evening.

The only people who qualified were Talya Northcott, Tottie Roundwood, and Vasile Bogdan. Talya had not come to the sponsors' marquee for a drink; she had been taken away by Mummy to have her wounded pride soothed with assurances that she would have made a much better Viola than Russ Lavery.

But Charles noticed his other two suspects were in the marquee talking together, and he edged through the crowd in their direction. Standing with his back to them, pretending interest in a poster-size Festival program, he listened to what they were saying.

"A triumph," Tottie Roundwood enthused. "He's got exactly what he wanted."

"Oh, yes," Vasile Bogdan agreed. "And I think we can confidently state that he wouldn't have got it without our help...don't you?"

NINETEEN

ONE NAME dominated the news pages of the next day's tabloids—Sally Luther. The death of a pretty actress—prettier in the archive photographs they reprinted from her sitcom heyday—was a good popular story.

Her career was recapitulated and analyzed. The days when her face was a fixture on the nation's television screens were recalled, together with tales of the fervor she inspired in her fans. At her peak she was the recipient of a massive postbag, including the usual creepy, obsessive letters that beautiful public faces inspire.

She'd even had the ultimate showbiz accolade of a stalker, who followed her around for some months. Unusually, in Sally Luther's case, she had been pursued and spied on by a woman rather than a man. Though this made her feel less threatened, it was still unnerving. Eventually she had called in the police, and her action had had the right effect: the pestering instantly ceased.

As well as recalling her career, the papers were lavish with tributes to Sally Luther from other showbiz names. The television executives who'd turned their backs during the eclipse of her popularity all came forward to say what a fine actress and delightful person she had been, how much they'd loved working with her, and how disappointed they'd be not to work with her again.

The circumstances of her death were described, but little detail was known, beyond the facts that she'd been taken ill onstage during rehearsal and died in hospital. One of the papers tried kite-flying the expression "mystery illness," but if they'd hoped that would give rise to speculation about AIDS, they had reckoned without the affection in which Sally Luther had been held. For the great British public, particularly after her death, she represented the squeaky-clean girl next door; they would never dream of associating her with something as squalid as AIDS.

But if Sally Luther had colonized the front of the papers, the arts pages were dominated by two names—Alexandru Radulescu and Russ Lavery.

The Asphodel production of *Twelfth Night* got an astonishing amount of coverage. Neither Pauline Monkton's cunning "targeting the right individuals" nor the additional interest given by Sally Luther's death was sufficient to explain the number of national critics who had been at the first night.

The reason was Alexandru Radulescu. He was, at least for a few months, the current vogue name, and no one who mattered in British theatre wanted to risk missing his latest production. Even if it meant forsaking the West End for the comparative wilds of Great Wensham, they had to be there. No doubt Radulescu and the Radulescu style would soon be condemned as "dated" and "meretricious," but during his brief moment in the sun he was the director who could do no wrong.

His revisualization of *Twelfth Night* was hailed as "mold-breaking," "daringly different," "a radical re-interpretation of what had always been thought of as a safe old play," and "an evening of pure theatre that challenges the spectator's every preconception."

Charles Paris could have spit.

He could understand an untutored audience going for Alexandru's flashy tricks, but he was amazed professional critics would be seduced by such modish claptrap. Surely they should respect Shakespeare's text and recognize when it was being traduced—that was their job, for God's sake! Critics should uphold the enduring values of the great British literary tradition, not be a prey to every new fad that comes along.

Even as he had the thought, Charles Paris realized how impossibly reactionary it sounded. Maybe he really was past his sell-by date. Maybe the values he represented were going the way of the dinosaurs. For a moment he was undermined by the appalling possibility that Alexandru Radulescu might be right.

But if the director was one of the golden boys of British theatre, there was another coming up fast to share the limelight. Russ Lavery had the kind of reviews even he—and his ego was of no mean proportions—would have been too bashful to write for himself.

The words *star* and *genius* were bandied about like small change. "A truly great Shakespearean performance," one critic enthused. "To be at Chailey Ferrars last night was to know what it must have been like to witness the debut of Garrick or Kean.''

Oh, for heaven's sake, thought Charles. What is going on here? He would never be able to understand the random cycle of critical opinion. He had rehearsed many shows he thought excellent, then seen them suffer savage dismemberment by the critics. He had been in productions he regarded as total shit, which had received rose-scented notices. It made no sense at all.

All he knew about criticism was that the only reviews he remembered were the bad ones. Over the years he must have had a good few laudatory notices—come on, he *must* have done—but all that stayed with him were of a type with the one he'd once received from *Plays & Players:* ''Charles Paris was also in the cast, though why is a question which neither the director nor the playwright seemed prepared to address.''

THE CAST were given the chance of a lie-in on the Wednesday morning, but there was a rehearsal call for two o'clock in the afternoon. The triumph of the first night had been the product of luck, adrenaline, and a sense of occasion. Details in the production still needed to be gone over and fixed.

Needless to say, most of these moments involved Russ Lavery. He was the one who, in his role as Viola, had suddenly taken on a lot of new scenes, and though his first-night performance had been stunning, at times he had been flying on a wing and a prayer.

Most of Viola's important scenes were with Orsino

or Olivia, so Sir Toby Belch and his cronies were not called for rehearsal till five o'clock. Charles Paris, who had risen after his landlady had stopped serving breakfast, reckoned that the late call justified a pub lunch.

He wandered out looking for the center of Great Wensham, but found that, in common with many other English country towns, its center had been removed. Where one might have expected a characterful town square was a brick-paved pedestrian shopping precinct, featuring Marks & Spencers, Currys, Next, the Body Shop, and all the chain-store names that appear in every other English town and city.

Still, he found a pub, Ye Olde King's Head, which looked as if its construction had been completed the day before. He bought a pint of beer, ordered a lasagna, and sat down with his drink. A compilation of hits of the sixties played just too loud in the background.

Damn, he'd meant to buy a *Times*. Then he could have had a go at the crossword until his food came. Without a paper, though, he couldn't avoid thinking about Sally Luther's death.

He was convinced she had been murdered, poisoned by a fatal injection pushed through the hessian screen in the wings at Chailey Ferrars.

He was also convinced that her death was the culmination of a sequence of poisonings. Gavin Scholes, John B. Murgatroyd, Sally Luther.

The question was, who had gained from that sequence of events? The obvious beneficiary of Gavin's removal had been Alexandru Radulescu, who took over the production of *Twelfth Night*. But the director could not have been directly responsible for the first poisoning because he had been nowhere near Chailey Ferrars when it happened.

The idea of Radulescu's having someone doing his dirty work for him, though, was quite appealing. And if he had had an accomplice, then the obvious candidate for the role was Vasile Bogdan. That would certainly explain the conversation Charles had overheard in the gents at the Willesden rehearsal room.

But when Gavin's poisoning was considered in conjunction with Sally Luther's death, the main beneficiary was undoubtedly Russ Lavery. Because of those two events, he had achieved the Sebastian/Viola double role that had restored his credibility as a stage actor. Was it possible that such an outcome had been planned from the start?

But Russ hadn't been at Chailey Ferrars either. Indeed, he had made a great public scene about not wanting to go to Chailey Ferrars. Could all that fuss have been deliberately set up to distance the actor from anything that might happen there?

If Russ was involved in Gavin's poisoning, then he too would have needed an accomplice. Maybe Vasile Bogdan fitted that role too...? It was Russ Lavery, Gavin had told Charles, who recommended Vasile as a suitable member of the company. Had there been a mutual exchange of favors between the two actors?

Or were they both involved in a conspiracy with Alexandru Radulescu?

The element that didn't fit into any of these possible

scenarios was the poisoning of John B. Murgatroyd. In rehearsal he'd been proving unreceptive to the director's ideas, but surely that wasn't sufficient reason to have him removed? The only person who had benefited directly from John B.'s illness was Chad Pearson, who inherited the role of Sir Andrew Aguecheek, but Charles had great difficulty including Chad in any list of suspects.

On the other hand...suppose John B. had been right when he suggested that his poisoning had been a mistake...? And that its intended victim had been Charles Paris...?

That was a chilling thought, which prompted another even more frightening.

Suppose Sally Luther's death had also been a mistake...?

At the time she was stabbed with the syringe, she shouldn't have been in the wings anyway. She was only there, sheltering from the rain, while they waited for Charles Paris, who had missed his cue.

The person who should have been there in that cramped space, pressed against the damp hessian, was Charles Paris himself.

Now the sequence of crimes had a logic. Gavin Scholes had been poisoned so that Vasile Bogdan would have the director he wanted. To get the part he wanted, Vasile'd have to remove Charles Paris. He'd made one attempt at the Indian restaurant, and another during the tech run. On each occasion he had caught the wrong victim.

But he was unlikely to let that stop him from trying again.

Charles Paris's lasagna was delivered to his table. He looked down at the greasy yellow, microwaved slabs, and he didn't feel hungry.

TWENTY

THE RAIN DID NOT return and the Wednesday evening was idyllically warm.

It was positively hot in the caravan dressing room as they waited for the Beginners call. Charles felt uncomfortable in his thick Sir Toby Belch costume. He also felt uncomfortable because Vasile Bogdan was there too. Still, no immediate danger—they weren't alone together. Russ Lavery, Benzo Ritter, and Tottie Roundwood were also present, lounging round, pretending they weren't nervous and glancing idly through the newspaper reports of Sally Luther's death.

"Dreadful business, isn't it?" said Charles for want of something else to say.

The others agreed it was.

"She was so young."

Russ Lavery, wearing a dress for Viola's first appearance in Illyria and sitting in a neat feminine pose, nodded uneasily. "Kind of thing happens too often for my liking. Chum of mine, only my age, just got married, suddenly keeled over a couple of months back. Heart attack. Dreadful."

From the nodding reactions of the others, it seemed no one thought there was anything suspicious about Sally's death. But, since he'd raised the subject,

Charles dared to probe a little further. "I wonder what she died of?"

"Heart? Brain tumor?" Tottie Roundwood suggested. "Usually one of those when it's as unexpected as that."

"What do you think, Vasile?"

The only reaction Charles got was a shrug of the shoulders.

He decided to be even braver. "Funny nobody's suggested the possibility of foul play."

"Foul play?" Benzo Ritter echoed.

"Yes, foul play. Murder."

"Don't be morbid, Charles," said Tottie mildly.

Vasile Bogdan's reaction was anything but mild. "That's a filthy suggestion!" he stormed. "The poor girl's not been dead two days. What on earth made you say that, you bloody fool?"

He'd gone too far. Charles tried to ease the situation with a *Twelfth Night* quotation: "'Now Mercury endue thee with leasing, for thou speak'st well of fools'."

Vasile, about to come back with a fierce rejoinder, was stopped by a tap on the caravan door. "Act one Beginners, please." And they all trooped out for the opening dumb show.

THANKS TO THE day's newspaper coverage—both sensational and artistic—all of the fixed seats for *Twelfth Night* were taken and spectators on folding chairs and rugs were densely spread over the surrounding slopes. Some of the audience that evening found the production a bit bizarre—it wasn't Shakespeare's play as they knew it—but the newspaper critics had told them it was good, so it must be. Anyway, they all enjoyed their picnics.

Charles Paris was very wary throughout the performance, watchful whenever Vasile Bogdan was in sight, and watching out for him when he wasn't. He knew he had to find some proof to back up his suspicions, and a plan was forming in his head as to how he might achieve that.

The show was a bit second-nightish. The audience wouldn't have noticed anything amiss, but the cast knew they hadn't quite scaled the peaks of the previous performance. There had been an inevitable sense of anticlimax, which many of the company proposed to counteract by a meal at the Great Wensham Tandoori.

Charles Paris, mindful of what had happened after the last communal Indian meal, and with his own plans for the rest of the evening, said he wouldn't join them. Nobody made any attempt to dissuade him from his decision.

In the cramped caravan, he removed the Sir Toby Belch costume and put on his street clothes. He felt the reassuring weight of a half-bottle of Bell's in his jacket pocket. What he was planning to do could well require some Dutch courage. In the other pocket were a pencil torch and a screwdriver.

Charles got a lift with the rest of the company in the Festival minibus, which stopped outside the Great Wensham Tandoori. Studiedly dilatory in getting out of the bus, he was able to check who went into the restaurant.

He ticked off Alexandru Radulescu, Vasile Bogdan, and Tottie Roundwood in the crowd that passed through the door. Good, that gave him at least an hour while they had their meal.

An hour, Charles reckoned, would be long enough. He reached into his pocket for the half-bottle of Bell's and prepared to snap the seal, but found the metal cap already loose. Dear oh dear, he must have had a swig earlier. Never mind. He braced himself with another long swallow.

THE HOUSE that Tottie, Vasile, and Alexandru were renting was on the outskirts of the town, conveniently without near neighbors. Charles had been prepared to use his screwdriver to force a lock or break a pane, but fortunately he found a downstairs window insecurely latched. Carelessness seemed to accompany hot weather.

After another emboldening swallow of Bell's, Charles Paris was quickly inside. His pencil torch showed he was in the sitting room. He moved through to the hall and up the stairs. Though not certain what he was looking for, he felt sure he was most likely to find it upstairs.

There were four doors—presumably three bedrooms and a bathroom—leading off the small landing. Charles opened one and flashed his pencil light across the room.

His eyes were immediately caught by a pile of

books on the bedside table. Drawn by the line of his torch beam, he approached them.

One looked ominously familiar. Light reflected from the dull gold lettering on the green spine. "Hay—*British Fungi.*"

The other books were more authorities on the same subject. Charles took a triumphant swig from his Bell's bottle. He felt vindicated. There had to be something in this room that would positively incriminate Vasile Bogdan.

He swung his beam across the room to a rack of small opaque-glass jars. Each seemed to contain a dry powder and was neatly labeled in a calligraphic hand. He moved forward to read the contents.

Aconite, Arsenic, Belladonna… Good God! He just had time to register that he'd found an entire poisoner's armory before his attention was snatched away by something behind the rack.

A dress drooping from a coat hanger.

He moved the torch beam round, revealing more dresses, skirts, and blouses, some of which he recognized. The dressing table was littered with pots of face cream and makeup.

He was in Tottie Roundwood's room.

Just as he formulated this thought, Charles Paris heard the sound from downstairs of the front door opening.

TWENTY-ONE

HE CAUGHT the strong whiff of Indian food before he heard the voices. Damn, he should have considered the possibility of their having a take-away. Still, presumably they'd eat in the dining room or kitchen. That should give him a chance to make a dash for it out of the front door.

"Shall we eat this upstairs?" said a voice, dashing his hopes. It was Tottie Roundwood who had spoken, but a new Tottie Roundwood. The voice was sultry, even sexy.

"Have we got a corkscrew?" asked a male voice Charles also instantly recognized.

"No need," she replied. "This Italian plonk has a screw-top."

"Good. Upstairs we go then."

The landing light was switched on, sending a blade of brightness across the room where Charles cowered. The smell of their take-away came ahead of the footsteps mounting the stairs. He looked desperately round. There was a window, but he didn't fancy launching himself into the dark from the first floor.

Hide under the bed, that was the only answer. Just as he'd done in that terrible adaptation of a French farce, *Follow Me, Fifi!* ("about as funny as an attack of shingles"—*Western Evening Press*).

Charles was under the bed with a faceful of dust before he remembered what had happened next in *Follow Me, Fifi!* A couple had come in, lain down on the bed, and started making love.

The footsteps paused on the landing. There was the sound of a long, succulent kiss.

''Your place or mine?'' Tottie Roundwood's voice asked throatily.

Oh, God, thought Charles, please. This isn't a French farce I'm involved in; it's a case of murder.

After a pause that seemed endless, the man replied, ''Mine. We can enjoy my music, yes?''

''Yes.'' Tottie chuckled. ''Amongst other things.''

The footsteps moved across the landing, away from Charles. A door opened and closed.

He gave it five minutes, then eased himself out from under the bed. There was dust all over him, he knew, but that was the least of his worries. He ran his torch beam once again over the books about fungi and the set of small jars. Making a quick decision, he pocketed the one labeled *Aconite*. Then he edged his way toward the door.

It creaked at the first gentle pull, and Charles froze. But there was no reaction from across the landing. He drew the door to him and stood exposed by the light.

He took a step toward the stairs. Still nothing. From the closed door opposite came the sound of Gregorian chant.

That was not the only sound, though. In profane counterpoint to the music, Charles could hear the mutual gasps of a couple making love.

He paused for a moment close to the door. A moan from Tottie changed into a little shriek. "Oh, you are a wonderful lover," she murmured. "These last six months have been the best time of my life, Alex."

WITH GREAT CARE, Charles moved down the stairs and across the hall. He turned the latch on the front door and closed it gingerly behind him, then padded softly off down the garden path.

His caution was probably unnecessary. Tottie Roundwood and Alexandru Radulescu sounded far too involved in each other to be aware of anyone else.

At the end of the street, Charles Paris slipped the half-bottle out of his pocket and rewarded himself with a substantial swig of Bell's.

He deserved it. Now at last he had some solid proof of wrongdoing. He didn't know much about the subject, but felt pretty sure that aconite derived from some form of poisonous fungus.

He also had a new suspect. If Tottie Roundwood had been having an affair with Alexandru Radulescu for the past six months, a great many previously inconsistent details fell into place. There is little a besotted woman nearing her fifties won't do to keep the affections of a younger lover.

Charles wondered how much Alexandru had been involved in the planning. Or had it been a Thomas à Becket scenario? Did Alexandru just intimate the outcome he desired and leave Tottie to make it happen?

The director must have been in contact with Asphodel, so that he knew they wanted to work with him.

Then he just tipped the wink to Tottie, and she got Gavin Scholes out of the way. Vividly the picture came back to Charles of the dining room at Chailey Ferrars, and the actress forcing a mushroom tartlet into the first director's mouth.

Then perhaps Alexandru had intimated that he was getting tired of Charles Paris's intransigence about how Sir Toby Belch should be played? Which had led to the poisoning in the Indian restaurant?

Unless... A new thought came to Charles. The scene at the restaurant was suddenly very clear to him. When John B. Murgatroyd had received his wrong order, he had called out down the table, "Anybody fancy swapping a chicken *dupiaza* for something stronger?"

And amongst the raucous responses, someone had shouted back, "I've already got one." Now, suddenly, Charles knew that that voice had been Sally Luther's.

In other words, the poisoning of John B. Murgatroyd had not been aimed at Charles Paris. It had been the first attempt on the life of Sally Luther.

It had failed, but the second, the injection of poison at Chailey Ferrars, had succeeded. Probably all Alexandru had said was, "Wouldn't it be great if I could actually have Russ Lavery playing both parts?" And Tottie Roundwood, unhinged by her infatuation, had taken the hint.

Another detail fell into place. Amidst all the upheaval that followed Sally Luther's death, Charles had forgotten the woman he had seen hurrying through the rain when he was on his way from Moira Handley's

Portacabin to the stage. But now that image too was crystal clear to him.

It must have been the murderer he had seen. Vasile Bogdan immediately left the reckoning. Even if he had been disguised in women's clothes, he was far too tall.

But the height and the gender were absolutely right for Tottie. True, Charles'd caught a glimpse of blond hair spilling from the anorak hood, but what actress doesn't have access to a range of wigs? She must have committed the crime only moments before, stabbed Sally through the hessian, and been running away from the scene.

And if that was the case, then—

But his thought processes were suddenly halted. With no warning at all, he was seized by violent nausea.

And as the entire contents of his stomach—and what felt like most of the stomach itself as well—spurted out of his mouth onto the pavement, one of Olivia's lines from *Twelfth Night* resonated in his head: "How now! Even so quickly may one catch the plague?"

But quotation immediately gave place to one appalling, heretical thought in Charles Paris's mind.

Somebody's poisoned my Bell's!

TWENTY-TWO

HE WAS LUCKY. The violence of his vomiting saved him from worse harm, flushing his body out as effectively as a stomach pump.

But it left him drained and feeble, slumped on the pavement. He was glad the good burghers of Great Wensham kept sober hours. They would not welcome dust- and puke-covered strangers littering their tidy streets.

THE DESK SERGEANT at the police station to which he staggered wasn't very welcoming either. The sight of a dust-and puke-covered stranger presenting him with a half-bottle of Bell's, a jar of powder, and some garbled story about a serial poisoner brought out his highest level of skepticism.

And D.I. Dewar, the bored-looking detective to whom Charles was passed over, looked equally disbelieving.

"So let me get this right, Mr....Parrish was it?"

"Paris."

"Paris then. You are saying that the contents of this bottle have been adulterated with some fungoid poison?"

"So I believe."

"And that it was done deliberately by someone trying to kill you?"

"Yes."

"When would they have had the opportunity to put the poison in the bottle?"

"It was in my jacket pocket hanging in the dressing room right through the performance."

"And you weren't there all the time?"

"No, I was *acting,* for heaven's sake." Surely that'd be obvious even to someone who didn't know anything about the theatre.

The detective gave him a look that suggested raising his voice hadn't been a good idea. Charles didn't care that much what the detective thought. He felt ill and weak; all he wanted to do was crawl into a warm bed.

The detective tapped his pencil on the desk tetchily. "You implied you had an idea who this person who's trying to kill you might be?"

Charles gave an ambivalent shrug.

"But you're not going to share your suspicions with me?"

"No."

"Why not?"

A good question, and yet Charles didn't yet feel certain enough to point a finger at Tottie Roundwood. In spite of the chain of logic he had worked out, she might still somehow turn out to be innocent, and it can prove tricky to mend fences with someone you've accused of murder.

No, it would be better to go one step at a time—

first get the whiskey tested for the poison, then look for the culprit.

"I'm not absolutely sure who it is," Charles replied evasively.

"You mean there are a lot of people it could be?"

"Well…"

The detective had his little joke. "Have a habit of making yourself unpopular with your workmates, do you, Mr. Parrish?"

"Look, I'm sure there is something criminal going on. I think it's related to Sally Luther's death too."

"Really?" Now he had got the detective's attention. "That case is currently under investigation, Mr. Parrish."

"You mean you've got proof that she was poisoned too?"

But Charles's eagerness was quickly slapped down. "Listen, if you think I'm about to give you information on the state of an investigation, then you have a very false idea of how we in the police force go about our business. Miss Luther's death was unexpected, so a postmortem was required. We will be kept informed of any developments that may concern us."

And that was all the detective would give. His attitude remained wary. There was a strong chance he was dealing with a crank. He had an instinctive distrust of theatre people, which Charles's appearance and unlikely story had done little to dispel.

D.I. Dewar did grudgingly, however, say he'd arrange for the contents of the bottle and the jar to be analyzed. He took the address of Charles's digs, confirmed how long the company was going to be in Great Wensham, and said he'd be in touch.

Charles felt so weak he called a cab to take him back. Inside his digs, he lay on the bed in his clothes and instantly passed out.

HE STAYED IN the following morning. For one thing, he was still feeling very battered after the poisoning. His throat burned and his stomach muscles felt as though they had been pulled inside out.

He was also not keen to get back among the *Twelfth Night* company until he had to. Whoever had poisoned the whiskey—and he was assuming it had been Tottie Roundwood—was going to realize that he had escaped and might well be moved to make another attempt on his life.

And he was hoping to hear something from the police before he had to go out to Chailey Ferrars for the evening's performance. Once the poison in the whiskey had been identified, then the whole machinery of official criminal investigation could be set in motion, and Charles Paris would cease to be under threat.

He tried to read a book and toyed with the crossword, but his thoughts kept slipping past the words. He wanted to talk to someone. Frances. But it was term-time. She could be pretty frosty if he called her at work without good reason. He wondered gloomily whether he had condemned himself to an eternal frost from his wife.

He couldn't concentrate; he kept coming back to Tottie Roundwood. How much of what had happened had she planned? Had she known from the start that Alexandru wanted to direct *Twelfth Night* with Russ Lavery playing the double role, or had the elements of her plan come together piecemeal? How had she got into the company in the first place?

Well, that at least was a question he could get answered. And it would give him something to do. He went to the phone and dialed Gavin Scholes's number.

The new wife answered. In an appropriately hushed voice, she said, "Yes, I'm sure he'd like to talk to you. But not for too long. Be careful you don't tire him. Phone for you, Gavin," she called out.

Another extension was picked up. "Hello?"

"Morning, Gavin, it's Charles Paris." Then, unthinking, he asked, "How are you?"

"Not so bad, all things considered," the director replied nobly. "It's quite a relief, actually, to have had it confirmed."

"Had what confirmed?"

"Oh, didn't you know?" Then, with considerable pride, he announced, "I've got cancer."

"Oh. Gavin. I'm so sorry." The condolence came out automatically, but Charles's mind was already racing with the implications of the news.

"That's very kind of you, Charles." A great complacency came into Gavin's voice. "I was pretty certain that's what it was from the start, but my consultant just wasn't convinced. Goodness, the barrage of tests I've been through—you just wouldn't believe it. I mean, first I had to—"

"Gavin, are you saying that it was cancer you were taken ill with after that day at Chailey Ferrars?"

"Yes, of course I am. Stomach cancer. That's what I told my consultant straightaway. But would he listen? *Now* of course he's very apologetic and says he should have paid more attention to me from the start, and he's moving heaven and earth to get the radiotherapy under way, but . . ."

Charles did not manage to get off the phone for half an hour. For a hypochondriac such as Gavin Scholes the diagnosis of a life-threatening disease was a vindication of his entire life. No one could doubt him anymore. He really was ill.

In the event, Charles didn't ask about how Tottie Roundwood had come into the *Twelfth Night* company. It didn't seem relevant.

Because if Gavin Scholes had been ill with cancer from the start, then he hadn't been poisoned at Chailey Ferrars. His inability to continue as director had been purely accidental.

And the logic of the case Charles Paris had been building against Tottie Roundwood fell apart totally.

TWENTY-THREE

"Mr. Parrish?"

"Paris."

"Yes. This is Detective Inspector Dewar from Great Wensham. We met last night."

"Right."

"I'm calling because we've had the lab results on the items you brought in."

"Yes?" Charles was tense. After the collapse of all his previous thinking about Tottie Roundwood's involvement in the case, he was fully prepared to be dismissed as a self-dramatizing crank. The skeptical tone from the other end of the phone was not encouraging.

"Well, let's start with the powder in the jar. That was indeed a preparation made from a vegetable substance—"

"Yes?"

"—though not in fact from a fungus."

"Oh. But aconite is a poison, isn't it?"

"Can be. What was found in that jar, however, would have purely medicinal applications."

"Oh."

"Something to do with homeopathic medicine. Not a subject on which I'm an expert, Mr. Parrish."

"Nor me." Though he knew that Tottie Roundwood was. He shivered at the thought of how close he'd come to making public accusations against her.

"No. However, Mr. Parrish, it appears that while the plant from which this powder originated is potentially poisonous, at the concentration in which it appears here, it is completely harmless. Or even, I suppose, beneficial, if you happen to be one of those weirdos who believes in homeopathic medicine."

The skepticism had given way to downright contempt. "Now we come on to the contents of the whiskey bottle."

Charles prepared himself for a serious dressing-down about wasting police time and being a hysterical theatrical crackpot. But, to his surprise, D.I. Dewar continued, "Traces of poison *were* found there, Mr. Parrish."

"A vegetable-based poison?"

"No, no. A chemical poison. Mercuric chloride." There was a silence. "It seems you had a very lucky escape, Mr. Parrish."

"Yes. And it also seems pretty definite that we have a poisoner in the *Twelfth Night* company, doesn't it?"

The detective was too canny to commit himself to an opinion on the subject. "What makes you say that?"

"Well, when you put what's happened to me—or nearly happened to me—together with Sally Luther's death…" D.I. Dewar did not react. "Come on, the two must be connected, mustn't they?"

"Must they?" Dewar was not giving anything

away. "Clearly, Mr. Parrish, we need to talk to you further."

"Yes. When?"

"Right away."

"The problem with that is"—Charles Paris looked at his watch—"it's now five forty-five. I have to be at Chailey Ferrars in three-quarters of an hour to get ready for tonight's performance of *Twelfth Night*."

"Mr. Parrish, if you're suggesting that a *play*"— the word was larded over with distaste—"should take precedence over a police investigation…"

"I'm not. I'm fully aware of how serious this is. All I'm saying is that if I'm not there for the performance because I'm being interviewed by the police, it will cause very considerable disruption—and will also provide a warning to any guilty person in the company that your investigation is drawing close."

There was a silence before D.I. Dewar conceded, "You may have a point, Mr. Parrish."

"So that means you do think someone in the company is guilty?"

But again the detective wouldn't be drawn. "What time does your play finish?"

"It comes down at ten-thirty."

"And at that time all of the company members will be around Chailey Ferrars?"

"Yes. Why, are you thinking of questioning everyone then?"

"Mr. Parrish…" The detective's stock of patience was quickly becoming depleted. "We are in the habit of conducting investigations in our own way. And we are not in the habit of providing information on how our investigations are going to irrelevant members of the public. We will speak again soon, Mr. Parrish.''

And the phone was put down with some force.

CHARLES HADN'T EATEN anything since his poisoning of the night before. To his surprise, when his landlady suggested some scrambled eggs before he went out to the show, the idea appealed.

She was a good landlady, with that quality that more landladies should manifest—unobtrusiveness. She brought his scrambled egg into the dining room and left him on his own to eat it. From a rack by the fire he picked up a copy of one of the previous day's broadsheet newspapers.

It was, inevitably, full of Sally Luther, but provided a less hysterical assessment of her importance than the tabloids had. Her death prompted a feature on the nature of media celebrity, in which one paragraph in particular caught Charles's attention.

Sally Luther also suffered from the disadvantages of being public property. She received a disturbing sequence of letters from an obsessed male fan, whose infatuation for her soured into violent fantasies. She also inspired the attentions of a young woman, who took to following her around at a distance for some months. Though Sally frequently tried to engage her in conversation, the girl always ran off when approached.

This was a nuisance, but little more. However,

the harassment became more worrying when Sally's pet cat was found poisoned. And then the mysterious girl began to stake out Sally's block of flats. The actress was justifiably unnerved by the sight every night of "a young blond woman, her face hidden by the hood of her anorak, standing immobile under the streetlamp opposite." Sally had been unwilling to call in the police before, but the new development changed her mind. Though the police never managed to catch the stalker, their presence ensured that the nuisance quickly ceased.

I wonder, thought Charles Paris. I wonder...

The image was vivid in his mind of a young woman hurrying through the rain, and a straggling wisp of blond hair escaping from a Mutual Reliable anorak.

TWENTY-FOUR

TALYA NORTHCOTT was sitting with a cup of coffee at a table in the shade of one of Chailey Ferrars' fine old oak trees. Now the weather had improved, a kind of literally green open-air "green room" had developed backstage. Evening sunlight dappled through the oak leaves, sparkling on Talya's fine blond hair and the silver brocade of her Olivia's Handmaiden costume.

Charles Paris, in his Sir Toby Belch gear, took a seat beside her. "Lovely evening, isn't it?"

"Oh, yes."

"Twenty minutes till Beginners."

"Mm..."

"You enjoying doing the show?"

Her mouth twisted into annoyance. "Not as much as I should be."

"Ah. Yes, of course." He had momentarily forgotten about her being the passed-over understudy for Sally Luther. "No, that was rotten luck. Don't worry, everyone in the theatre's had bad breaks from time to time." He grinned. "Me more than most maybe."

She gave him a look that suggested bad breaks for someone like him might be justified, but not for her. Mummy's solicitude had certainly produced one very spoiled and self-obsessed young lady.

"Also, Talya, I mean, you must recognize that Russ Lavery is a *name*, and I'm afraid *names* count for a lot in this business."

"That's not the point. I was contracted to play Handmaiden to Olivia *and* to understudy all the female parts." She sniffed irritably. "I'm going to get on to my agent. I reckon Asphodel's in breach of contract."

"I don't know that making a fuss will do much good."

"Perhaps not, but *it'll make me feel better*," she said with considerable venom. "And what's so great about Russ Lavery, anyway? All right, he's in the telly series, and he plays that one part okay—not that it's very hard. But it's daft having him playing Viola. It goes absolutely against the text of Shakespeare's play."

In different circumstances Charles would have agreed with her and joined in a mutual moan about Alexandru Radulescu's massacre of *Twelfth Night*. But this wasn't the moment.

"You admired Sally very much, didn't you?" he probed gently.

"Yes. She was a role model for me. She was the kind of actress I want to be—and will be," she added, then went on resentfully, "She would have been much better as Viola than Russ will ever be. *I* would have been much better as Viola than Russ will ever be."

Charles was about to ask when she'd first met Sally, but Talya continued on another burst of anger. "It's not fair. I should be playing that part. After everything I've done, I should be playing that part!"

"When you say 'everything you've done'—"

But Talya Northcott was too infuriated to listen. "It's ridiculous that Viola should be played by some pathetic male television star with a drug problem!"

"With a drug problem?" Charles echoed.

Talya Northcott looked sheepish. She'd said more than she intended. But a what-the-hell defiance came into her face. "Yes. Russ Lavery's into hard drugs. I know." A thought came to her. "And I've half a mind to tell the press about his little habit.... That'd sort him out, wouldn't it? Really do something to his Mr. Clean image."

"What do you base your knowledge on?"

"I've *seen* him doing hard drugs."

"When?"

"The night of the tech. The night Sally died. After his first Sebastian/Antonio scene-act two, scene one—Russ came back into the caravan where I was and he was in a filthy mood—very tense and twitchy."

"Was it just you in the caravan?"

"No, I was there with Vasile and Chad."

"And how long did they stay there?"

"What?" She didn't like having her narrative interrupted. "What does that matter?"

"Please, just tell me."

An exasperated sigh. "All right, let me think... Well, Chad went to do his Clown bit in act two, scene three, and then Vasile was there till Fabian's first proper entrance—act two, scene five. You know that—you're in the scene, for God's sake!"

"Yes," Charles agreed meekly. "You were saying, about Russ...?"

"Right. Well, as I say, he came in after his scene in an absolutely vile mood, and he twitched around for a little while, and then he stormed out again. And the reason he did that was because he needed a fix."

"What makes you so sure?"

"Because I saw him. Out of the caravan window. He'd stopped under a tree out of the rain and I saw him pull something out of that pouch he has on his costume."

"What did he pull out?"

"It was a syringe."

"Ah," said Charles Paris. "Was it?"

TWENTY-FIVE

THAT NIGHT Sir Toby Belch went through the comic machinations of the first half of *Twelfth Night,* but the actor playing him was on automatic pilot. Charles Paris remained detached, his mind forging links in a new chain of logic.

With Gavin's illness explained, the two remaining crimes had clearly both been aimed at Sally Luther, and Russ Lavery was the one who had benefited most from her death. Alexandru Radulescu, as the current licensed iconoclast of the theatrical establishment, would have got the same reviews if she had remained alive. The doubling of Sebastian and Viola was just one more coup in a production full of innovation (or perversity, if you shared the Charles Paris view).

But for Russ it was a career-making change. Now, to add to the fame and money brought by television, he had the artistic respectability that only a high-profile theatrical performance can give. The value of that is incalculable and might well make an ambitious actor contemplate all kinds of criminality.

The more Charles thought about Russ, the more details fitted. He cast his mind back to Gavin Scholes's production of *Macbeth* at Warminster. Fresh out of the Webber Douglas School of Acting, Russ Lavery had been callow and naive. He had also attached himself

with doglike devotion to an older actress, the somewhat precious Felicia Chatterton.

Was it fanciful to imagine that that was not his first
comparable infatuation? At a younger age might not
the hypersensitive Russ Lavery have become similarly
fixated on Sally Luther?

Because, as Charles watched Russ onstage as Viola,
he was struck again by how superbly the actor played
a woman. It wasn't just mannerism; he seemed to take
on complete female identity. The ease with which he'd
done that, from the first experimental moment of role-
swapping in rehearsal, suggested that he had practice
in cross-dressing.

And that would explain the incongruity of Sally Luther having been followed by a woman all those
months. Surely with stalkers it was a sex thing. In the
famous examples of such incidents, the actresses had
always been pestered by men.

Mentally Charles kicked himself. He should have
thought of this earlier. After nearly a month of Alexandru Radulescu's harping on sexual ambivalence, his
mind should have made the jump more readily. It was
all there in *Twelfth Night;* the whole play was about
the ambiguity of gender.

Charles had planned to confront Russ Lavery at the
end of the show, but two factors made him move his
plans forward.

The first was his own danger. The confirmation that
Charles's half-bottle of Bell's had been poisoned also
confirmed that the murderer saw him as a threat. After
one failure, another attempt on his life seemed a cer-

tainty. And Sir Toby Belch had an uncomfortable amount of booze-swigging to do throughout the play. To poison the contents of his tankard in the wings would not be difficult. Charles gave himself a mental note under no circumstances to let any of the fluid he was meant to quaff touch his lips.

The other pressure on his plans was the appearance of Detective Inspector Dewar backstage during the first half of *Twelfth Night*. Since he was in plain-clothes, there was little chance of anyone but Charles knowing his mission. When, however, a message went out during the interval requesting all the company and crew to assemble briefly at the end of the show, Charles reckoned the murderer might become suspicious that someone was onto him.

There was also pride at stake. Charles Paris had got so far down the road of investigation that, for his own satisfaction, he wanted to have his theory proved correct. The police could then move in and arrest the culprit, but Charles didn't want them to upstage him by having their denouement first.

No, he would have his confrontation during the interval.

THAT AUGUST the evenings remained warm even after the sun had gone down, and few of the cast chose to spend their interval in the stuffy caravans. They sat outside in the alfresco "green room" or lolled on the grass. The long interval was still a bone of contention. It was hard to keep up concentration, and they looked forward to moving on to the studio theatre in Norwich, where the running of *Twelfth Night* would not be dictated by the demands of picnickers.

Russ Lavery, who, because of his onerous double role, was more concerned about threats to his concentration than most, habitually sat quietly in one of the caravans for the full duration of the interval; and it was there that Charles Paris found him.

Russ looked up without enthusiasm. He had a glass of mineral water and an open copy of the play in front of him. "I'm concentrating. What do you want, Charles?"

"I want to talk about Sally Luther's death."

A sigh. "I'd have thought everything to be said on that subject had already been said."

"The police are investigating it, you know."

"So? They'd be likely to investigate any unexplained death, wouldn't they?"

Russ Lavery sounded very calm, as if he had deliberately damped down his pulse and heart rate to improve his concentration.

"They think it was murder." Charles hadn't actually had that in as many words from D.I. Dewar, but he thought the implication was clear.

"Huh. Someone always thinks every unexplained death is murder. But why would anyone want to murder Sally? Was she screwing some other woman's husband, or what?"

If this was a pretense of innocence, it was a convincing one. But then, Charles reminded himself, he was dealing with a consummately good actor.

"There are other motives than sexual jealousy."

"I'm sure there are." Russ now sounded simply bored.

"Professional jealousy, for example. Or professional advantage."

"I don't know what you're talking about."

"Russ, when did you first meet Alexandru Radulescu?"

"Hm? I don't know. Six months ago...?"

"And did you talk together about *Twelfth Night* then?"

"We talked about a lot of plays. Alex has got a lot of exciting ideas."

"But did the idea of doing *Twelfth Night* with Sebastian and Viola doubling come up then?"

"I can't remember. It may have done."

"Did it?"

"Yes, I think it did. Just as a speculative idea. I certainly never thought it'd happen."

"But now it has happened..."

"Yes."

"...thanks to Sally Luther's death."

"Yes." Russ Lavery was silent for a moment as the idea took root. "Good God. You're not suggesting Alex killed her, are you?"

"No, I'm not."

"Then I don't see what you're talking about, Charles." Russ looked genuinely puzzled.

"Russ, on the evening of Sally's death, you were seen holding a syringe..."

Up till this point Russ Lavery's cool had been unchallenged, but Charles's words really shook him.

"Oh, God," he murmured. "How did you find out? You didn't see me."

"No, somebody else did."

"Look, Charles, you mustn't shop me about this." Now there was a naked plea in Russ's voice.

"Why shouldn't I?"

"Because it'd ruin my career."

"Yes, I think it probably would," Charles agreed evenly.

"But you don't know the pressures that drive someone to that kind of thing. Oh, yes, I've been doing well the last few years, and everyone's jealous and thinks what a lucky fellow Russ Lavery is. But in this business doing well is not good enough. You have to do *better* all the time, have something new on the horizon, always be moving on.

"So, yes, at the moment they're still talking of further series for *Air-Sea Rescue,* but the ratings only have to fall half a million and they'll pull the plugs on it as quick as breathing. Look what happened to Sally's series—just suddenly, thank you very much, good-bye. And actors who haven't got something else lined up when that happens can have a very sticky few years."

"So is that why you did it?"

"Yes. It made me feel better."

"Really?"

"And it still does make me feel better. Look!"

Suddenly Russ Lavery pulled up the sleeve of his doublet. The reason for his tantrum with the wardrobe mistress was now clear. He didn't dare to show a fore-

arm that was a wasteland of scars and punctures. ''I'm
ruining my body. I'm putting my life at risk. But it
does make me feel better! Without this my whole life's
a mess. With it I can just about cope.''

''Ah. Right. That's what you used the syringe for?''

''Yes. What else?''

''And Sally Luther...?''

''Sally Luther wasn't into drugs.'' Russ's bewilder-
ment was so genuine that Charles's suspicions crum-
bled away. ''No, she somehow managed to cope with
all the pressure...when it was all happening...and during the even more difficult time—when it all started
to fall apart. I admired her for that because I'm
afraid...when it all goes wrong for me—and it will, it
will, it does for everyone...well, I'm worried that I'll
just do more of this.'' He gestured feebly at his ravaged arm.

Charles Paris looked at the handsome wreck in front
of him. Russ Lavery wasn't a murderer, just an actor
paying the price of his celebrity. That was what Sally
Luther had done too, though in a different way. She
had died because she had inspired too much public
affection. Russ Lavery was killing himself because of
his fear that the public affection he inspired would one
day trickle away.

There are times, Charles Paris thought, when there's
a lot to be said for being an unsuccessful actor.

TWENTY-SIX

SIR TOBY BELCH had to do his first scene of the second half, act 3, scene 2, before Charles Paris could go into action. He found D.I. Dewar waiting in the administrative-office Portacabin. Moira Handley was not there, though another detective was.

"You're not watching the show?"

The curt head-shake showed exactly what the inspector thought of the theatre.

"Listen," said Charles. "I've got an idea..."

The two detectives looked skeptical, but did at least hear him out.

"I'm very doubtful it'll work," said D.I. Dewar finally.

"But isn't it worth trying? It can't do any harm, can it?"

The inspector was silent for a moment, then conceded, "Well, I suppose not. All right, you can have a go."

"I mean, who have you talked to so far? Who does actually know why you're here?"

"Just the company manager."

"Oh," said Charles. "If you told him, then probably everyone *does* know already."

But they didn't seem to. Certainly all the cast members to whom he murmured in the wings why they were being asked to stay after the show seemed surprised at the news. Mind you, he had to mention it to only a couple to ensure that everyone knew.

A great while ago the world begun,
*   With hey, ho, the wind and the rain:*
But that's all one, our play is done,
*   And we'll strive to please you every day.*

The sitar player's enunciation had improved over the run, and the final moment of *Twelfth Night* still retained its magic. The Great Wensham audience, having greatly enjoyed their picnics, erupted into applause.

As the cast came forward to do their curtain calls, Charles counted them. All present and correct. If the murderer was going to make a move, it hadn't happened yet.

The cast had been told to get out of their costumes and reassemble onstage as quickly as possible. Charles, as he had arranged with D.I. Dewar, stayed in his Sir Toby Belch gear and hurried down the side of the auditorium to the box office, a rectangular shed that stood by the gates into the theatre field.

The inspector was in there, looking out over the mass of Great Wensham folk trooping toward the car park laden with rugs and garden furniture. Overhead working lights beamed down on the faces as they passed. One or two were talking about *Twelfth Night;* the majority were discussing their picnics.

"If this doesn't work, it's a bloody waste of time," Dewar grumbled to Charles. "Or if the person we're looking for has already left."

"Everyone was at the curtain call."

"Hm. Well, we'll see…"

It was hard to concentrate on the individual faces that streamed past. Charles was tempted by a couple of blond heads, but neither looked quite right. D.I. Dewar's grumbling about time-wasting grew more vociferous.

Charles had almost given up when he saw what he had been hoping to see. The audience flow had dwindled to just a few stragglers. Besashed usherettes and Festival volunteers in Mutual Reliable anoraks milled around the seating, picking up rubbish, chatting and giggling.

And someone with their anorak hood up was walking briskly toward the exit. The face was hidden, but a wisp of blond hair escaped the hood.

"There," Charles murmured.

He slipped out of the box office and waited in the shadows beside it. Then, just when the hooded figure was about to pass, he stepped out into its path.

"Good evening," said Charles Paris.

The speed with which his throat was grabbed stunned him. He felt himself pushed back against the counter of the box office and could feel his assailant fumbling for something in his pocket.

In the glare of the working light he saw a syringe raised to stab at him.

"You bastard! This time you won't get away!" the murderer screamed.

Charles Paris closed his eyes.

"I'll have that, thank you very much."

It was D.I. Dewar's voice. Charles opened his eyes and saw his assailant's wrist caught in the inspector's viselike grip. The two arms swayed in conflict for a moment, as if wrestling.

Then the inspector's started to win. It forced the other down toward the box-office counter. As it drew close, it slammed the loser's hand against the wood.

There was a little cry as the syringe dropped, and Charles felt the pressure on his throat slacken.

He reached across and grabbed the free arm. The murderer was now held by D.I. Dewar across the box-office counter and by Charles from outside. In the struggle, the anorak hood slipped back, pulling the blond wig with it.

Charles found himself looking into the furious face of Benzo Ritter.

TWENTY-SEVEN

HIS ATTACK on Charles, witnessed by D.I. Dewar, was sufficient cause for the police to arrest the boy, and while he was in custody, his other crimes were investigated.

His handwriting was matched to the threatening letters Sally Luther had received at the height of her television fame. Faced with that fact, he confessed to everything.

Yes, he had been the "woman" who trailed the star. He loved her, he needed to be near her. But, he explained, he'd been very immature at the time. Later he realized that the only way to be with his idol was to earn her respect as an equal.

That was why he had gone into show business. When she met him as one of her profession rather than an anonymous admirer, he knew she was bound to succumb, to feel as much for him as he did for her.

But that was not what had happened. In the event, when he declared his passion, she had laughed at him. He couldn't tolerate that. Other people might find out, they might laugh at him too.

So it was only logical that Sally Luther would have to die.

He'd always been fascinated by poisons. Indeed, his school nickname "Benzo" had been based on an illicit experiment he'd done in the chemistry lab with nitro-benzene. Mind you, he told his interrogators proudly, he'd used atropine from belladonna when he'd poisoned Sally's cat.

He'd used the mercuric chloride in powder form in the Indian restaurant, surreptitiously shaking some over one of the chicken *dupiazas* in the confusion of the food's arrival. The fact that he had poisoned the wrong person he regarded as an inconvenience rather than a tragedy.

Then he had employed the same poison in solution to inject Sally Luther and adulterate the Bell's whiskey. His turning his murderous attentions to Charles Paris, it emerged, was due to another misunderstanding. A few days previously, Charles had raised the subject of Sally Luther's death in the dressing-room caravan. To defuse a potential confrontation with Vasile Bogdan, he had quoted from *Twelfth Night:* "Now Mercury endue thee with leasing, for thou speak'st well of fools!"

Benzo Ritter had taken this reference to "Mercury" as evidence that Charles knew the poison he was using, and that had led him to doctor the half-bottle of Bell's. The boy had been extremely irritated that Charles Paris survived that attempt.

At no stage during his questioning and subsequent trial did Benzo Ritter demonstrate any feelings of guilt or remorse.

At the trial, psychological reports ruled him to be insane, and he was committed to a secure institution.

BENZO RITTER'S ABSENCE made little difference to the Asphodel production of *Twelfth Night*. A new Second Officer was found and the play set off from Great Wensham on its triumphant tour.

Charles Paris did not enjoy the experience. His performance moved a little closer to what Alexandru Radulescu wanted, but felt uncomfortable to Charles, eternally marooned between two stools. He still longed to play Sir Toby Belch as Shakespeare had intended the part to be played, but didn't think he was likely ever to get another chance. As Moira Handley had said in a different context, the moment had passed.

Charles didn't really feel part of the tour. His resistance to the communal hero worship of Alexandru Radulescu isolated him. John B. Murgatroyd had been his closest ally in the company, and though the invalid made a full recovery from his poisoning, he did not rejoin the show. As *Twelfth Night* crisscrossed the United Kingdom—with a diversion to the Czech Republic—Charles Paris felt marginalized and lonely.

ALEXANDRU RADULESCU did not return to Romania, but stayed on to impose his personality and perversity on more classic English texts. He continued to be hailed as a genius, until one day a new enfant terrible took the British theatre by the scruff of its neck, and the Radulescu style seemed suddenly meretricious and old hat.

RUSS LAVERY'S CAREER went from strength to strength. He managed to combine television popularity with serious critical respect for his theatre work. And the British public adored him even more after his much-publicized battle with heroin addiction.

JULIAN ROXBOROUGH-SMITH added another artistic directorship to his portfolio. He was appointed to run the West Bartleigh Festival and, thereafter, in his usual dilettante fashion, spent his time rebooking the same artistes for all three festivals. Since he still acted as agent for many of these artistes, he made rather a good living.

And Moira Handley, needless to say, continued to do all the work.

GAVIN SCHOLES'S CANCER required surgery, granting him his lifelong wish of being able to talk about "my operation." It was followed by a course of radiotherapy, which seemed to work. He apparently made a complete recovery, though, as he kept telling his new wife—and anyone else incautious enough to listen— "it might just be a temporary remission."

CHARLES PARIS had intended to ring Frances during the tour, but somehow didn't get round to it.

Back in London it was early December and cold. Unequal to the upheaval of finding somewhere new, Charles had agreed with his landlord to continue at Hereford Road, paying the exorbitantly increased rent. The conversion from bed-sitter to studio flat had managed to keep the essential features of the original space—in other words, its total lack of charm.

There wasn't any work around either. He'd spoken to Maurice Skellern, who'd once again said that things were "very quiet." Charles watched what was left of the money he'd made from *Twelfth Night* slowly dwindle. He signed on again at the Lisson Grove Unemployment Office.

After a week of mooching round his bed-sitter—no, studio flat—he finally rang Frances. And he found she had exciting news.

"I'm doing an exchange program with a school in the States."

"What does that mean?"

"An American teacher comes over to my school and I go and teach in California for a year."

"Oh. When does this happen?" Charles asked bleakly.

"Starts in January."

"How was it arranged?"

"Through an American friend."

"The one you met at the international teachers' conference?"

"That's right."

"What, so he'll be over here while you're there, will he?"

"No, it's another member of staff I'm swapping with. My friend will be in California," Frances replied crushingly.

And once again it seemed inconceivable that things had ever gone well for Charles Paris.

CHARLAINE HARRIS

If the shoe fits ...

A man's body plummets from a low-flying plane onto the freshly manicured lawn of Aurora "Roe" Teagarden. When the corpse embedded in her backyard is identified as Detective Jack Burns, the town is abuzz. Everyone knows that Burns and Roe just plain disliked each other.

Message or warning? When another corpse and then an almost-dead body land in Roe's vicinity, it becomes clear that Aurora is once again in the middle of murder—and this time, it's personal.

DEAD OVER HEELS

"A rollicking whodunit."
—Buffalo News

First Time in Paperback

Available in January 1998 where books are sold.

An Aurora Teagarden Mystery

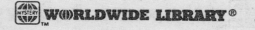

MYSTERY **WORLDWIDE LIBRARY**®

WCH260

BARBARA BURNETT SMITH

IN-LAWS...AND OUTLAWS.

The centennial celebration of Purple Sage, Texas, has arrived, but Jolie Wyatt isn't in much of a party mood: her in-laws are coming. And these nice people still wish their son was married to his first wife, an elegant English rose who has also returned to Purple Sage for the festivities.

But when a double shooting leaves a woman dead and the town's sheriff badly wounded, Jolie finds herself trying to clear the prime suspect: her husband. But she may be too late to save her own neck as her sleuthing draws her even closer to a killer.

First Time in Paperback

Celebration IN Purple Sage

A Jolie Wyatt Mystery

"Jolie's third case is hands-down her best..." —*Kirkus Reviews*

Available in January 1998 where books are sold.

shocking pink

THEY WERE ONLY WATCHING...

The mysterious lovers the three girls spied on were engaged in a deadly sexual game no one else was supposed to know about. Especially not Andie and her friends whose curiosity had deepened into a dangerous obsession....

Now fifteen years later, Andie is being watched by someone who won't let her forget the unsolved murder of "Mrs. X" or the sudden disappearance of "Mr. X." And Andie doesn't know who her friends are....

WHAT THEY SAW WAS MURDER.

ERICA SPINDLER

Available in February 1998 at your favorite retail outlet.

The Brightest Stars in Women's Fiction.™

MIRA